W9-BFM-596

GOTHIC!

BUSSELTON SENIOR HIGH SCHOOL LIBRARY

SENIOR HIGH SCHOOL

F GOT

LIBRARY

GOTHIC!

Ten Original Dark Tales

edited by Deborah Noyes

WALKER BOOKS

AND SUBSIDIARIES

LONDON · BOSTON · SYDNEY · AUCKLAND

These stories are works of fiction. Names, characters, places, and incidents are either the product of the author's imagination or, if real, are used fictitiously.

First published 2004 by Walker Books Ltd
87 Vauxhall Walk, London SE11 5HJ

2 4 6 8 10 9 7 5 3 1

Introduction © 2004 Deborah Noyes
Compilation © 2004 Deborah Noyes
"Lungewater" © 2004 Joan Aiken Enterprises, Ltd
"Morgan Roehmar's Boys" © 2004 Vivian Vande Velde
"Watch and Wake" © 2004 M. T. Anderson
"Forbidden Brides of the Faceless Slaves in the Nameless House of the Night
of Dread Desire" © 2004 Neil Gaiman
"The Dead and the Moonstruck" © 2004 Caitlín R. Kiernan
"Have No Fear, Crumpot Is Here!" © 2004 Barry Yourgrau
"Stone Tower" © 2004 Janni Lee Simner
"The Prank" © 2004 Gregory Maguire
"Writing on the Wall" © 2004 Celia Rees
"Endings" © 2004 Garth Nix

Cover illustration © 2004 Gary Kelley

This book has been typeset in M Joanna and Mithras ITC

Printed and bound in Great Britain by Bookmarque Ltd, Croydon, Surrey

All rights reserved. No part of this book may be reproduced, transmitted
or stored in an information retrieval system in any form or by any means,
graphic, electronic or mechanical, including photocopying, taping
and recording, without prior written permission from the publisher.

British Library Cataloguing in Publication Data:
a catalogue record for this book
is available from the British Library

ISBN 1-84428-253-8

www.walkerbooks.co.uk

For Valerie Noyes,
who kept the dark away —
but not completely

BUSSELTON SENIOR HIGH SCHOOL

LIBRARY

≈ CONTENTS ≈

INTRODUCTION

"The oldest and strongest emotion of mankind is fear," wrote the author H. P. Lovecraft, figurehead of the cult of "weird" fiction and arguably the biggest influence on horror and suspense writing since Edgar Allan Poe.

Fear.

Once bitten, our eyes dilate. Our hair stands on end. Our skin becomes goose flesh. Offered a frightening diversion, a child will cover her eyes and peek through her fingers. Don't show me. *Show me.* The heart thuds, and the blood races. Like the vampires that make it their hunting ground, the gothic tale is all paradox. It might scare us to death, but it also startles us to our senses, enlivens us; we take pleasure in terror.

Horace Walpole's novel *The Castle of Otranto* introduced what later came to be termed the "gothic romance" in 1764. His popular tale of a villain-hero inspired countless imitations and innovations, and since then writers of all kinds have lured readers with gothic themes and conventions. But what exactly, beyond a love for the supernatural and surreal, makes a story "gothic"?

For one thing, its preoccupation with bygone days. The gothic past is a prison of tyranny and superstition. It looms large, and its shadow blots out the present—hence family curses, ancient castles, crumbling parchments, decaying bodies, moaning ancestral portraits, and labyrinthine catacombs through which sinister aristocrats pursue vulnerable heroines. Classic gothic tales swarm with scheming heirs, dark twins, dread, claustrophobia, and persecution—all presented in an atmosphere of brooding suspense, almost always in the maddening confines of some ruined dwelling. There is melodrama, melancholy, and poetry to spare. Nature is no sympathetic reflection of human goodness—our Romantic link to the Divine—but a vile and twisted reflection of godless fears and anxieties. Flowers pulse with poison; ancient trees are savaged and split by lightning; and the final resting place for the body, the good earth, becomes a worm-plagued torture chamber for the soul. There is, of course, no shortage of graveyards, hauntings, bewitchings, and bitten necks, as well.

Does this mean a gothic tale is the same as a horror story? The differences may be academic, but it's probably more accurate to think of gothic as a room within the larger house of horror. Its décor is distinctive. It insists on the burden of the past. It also gleefully turns our ideas of good and evil on end. In horror stories, the boundaries between innocence and malevolence are often clearly marked in blood. In the gothic, evil frequently triumphs; beauty certainly fades; monks may be wicked and thrive; murderers can and do claim the moral high ground.

Not all the stories in this collection follow the gothic standard established by Horace Walpole. Some, like the fabulously eerie "Lungewater" and "Writing on the Wall," do have a classic feel. Others—"Morgan Roehmar's Boys," "Watch and Wake," and "The Prank," for instance—are more graphic and contemporary. Neil Gaiman's hilarious send-up is also what he calls a "love letter" to the form and celebrates the stubborn resilience of the human imagination. Barry Yourgrau, too, adds humor to the mix, while Janni Lee Simner, Caitlín Kiernan, and Garth Nix mine the fairy tale or dark fantasy for inspiration. All draw on a rich legacy that extends from Ann Radcliffe to Anne Rice, Poe to Stephen King, Bram Stoker to Lovecraft—with the added bonus that, taken together, the stories form a delicious sampler of dark fiction by some of the most talented authors writing today for young adults.

You may wonder, Why take a literary form that revels in rot and ruin and tailor it to you . . . teen readers? By its nature there's something gothic about coming of age, and a fair number of these stories treat that theme (and others that may be of interest: subversion and transgression; resistance, both passive and aggressive; alienation; the awareness of youth and beauty as transitory states . . .). You're young enough to glory in youth, after all, and old enough to grasp the inevitability of its going; conscious of your doom, ennobled by it even, you stand with Hamlet as much as with Frankenstein. What better audience for this bleak and lofty form, I thought— setting out to contact the authors in this book—than you, dear reader, on the dizzying brink of adulthood?

Contemporary Goth subculture has borrowed on gothic-lit themes, of course, but you don't have to listen to bands like Bauhaus or wear black to seek uneasy refuge in these pages. As the child in you knows, it's sweet to be scared, no matter who you are . . . so catch your breath.

Come in.

Deborah Noyes

LUNGEWATER

Joan Aiken

On Christmas Eve each year, for many years, I used to visit my great-aunt Theodosia, the last survivor of three aged sisters. And a long, dispiriting journey I was obliged to take, involving two bus changes and extended periods spent exposed in cheerless wayside bus shelters. And at the finish, a choice of walking, either up a straight, bleak stretch of windy road, or along a path that, though beautiful, was frightening (for reasons to be explained later), so I never went that way unless I had a companion with me.

One Christmas Eve, waiting for the third of my buses in a bus shelter with broken glass panes, a central bar missing from the bench, and various hate messages scribbled on the dented litter-bin, which was the only other furniture, I was accosted by a very singular old gentleman who came into the bus shelter and sat down on the other end of the damaged seat.

More than commonly tall, he was dressed in a Norfolk jacket and knickerbockers of an old-fashioned cut, made from some hairy, fawn-colored material, serge perhaps. He wore high canvas boots and long, thick, woolen stockings of the same sandy brown, and was quite bald, but this was compensated for by the long, thick, white beard and moustache that framed the lower part of his face like a garden hedge.

"Can you tell me, my young friend," he asked me in a heavy foreign accent, "is it from this place that I am to catch an omnibus to Hovel Hanger?"

I told him that, yes, it was, and that I was hoping to get the same bus myself but had been told it would be late owing to wintry road conditions.

"Ah, so? But I hope that we shall arrive at that place before too late in the day—before it grows dark."

His accent was very guttural—the h's in "hope" and "Hovel Hanger" came out with a thick "gh" sound, like blobs of ketchup from a bottle.

"To pass time, then, I shall relate to you the story of why I am come all the way from Dahoungarie to visit this small place."

"Thank you, sir. I should like to hear it," I said politely, hoping that the story would not be long and that the bus would soon come.

"I tell you the story of Count Hugo Boyanus, who fled from my country after the revolution there and came to settle in a house near Hovel Hanger. Before, he had possessed hundreds of miles of farmland and forest, besides coal mines, oil wells, factories, rivers full of fish, whole towns and villages and their inhabitants. Now—no more. No property left. But money, yes, that he did have; being a man of insight, he had seen trouble coming years earlier, so, wisely, he sent his gold abroad to mount up for him in foreign lands, in foreign banks. Then, when the people rose, and took away from the rich, Count Boyanus escaped and traveled to this country, with just one servant to carry his bags, a slave named Stiva."

"A slave?"

"Before, the count had owned hundreds of serfs—slaves, you would say; it is the same thing. Among them was this boy, Stiva, whose parents were dead. They, too, had been serfs, and had died in the count's service. The boy, Stiva, could neither read nor write. Had never been to school. What choice did he have? There was no one to speak up for him. When told to do so, he went with the count, though he was sad to leave home, and, in your country, he could not understand the language. Nor was there anyone to take his part. So he remained, unpaid, in the service of the count, who bought Lungewater manor house, near Hovel Hanger.

"In former days, the count had often traveled abroad. He spoke other tongues—English, French, Italian—with fluency. He had made friends in other lands. He was an educated man, a poet, a historian; he wrote with knowledge and elegance on many topics.

"But the boy, Stiva, remained an illiterate. Books, written words, meant nothing to him. Nor did he learn many words of your language. He had no time. All day he served the count. Carrying up his breakfast, polishing his boots, cleaning and oiling his bird guns (for the count was a great sportsman), fastening the flies on his fishing lines (for the River Lunge ran through the count's land).

"Now," said the old gentleman, "I come to tell the important part. The count was in love with an English lady. He had met her some years before when he was reading for a master's degree at Bad Hassenberg University. She was there with her mother, who was taking the waters. The town was very gay at that time. There were balls, riding parties; there was a casino and gambling—picnics, archery, horse racing. The lady was very young, very charming, light-hearted, beautiful as an angel. She did not, perhaps, take him too seriously. They rode, they danced, they walked together in the forests . . . but she was many years younger, and her family was not favorably disposed toward the count. They thought him too old, too foreign perhaps. But he had lost his heart entirely. When the lady's family returned to England, he lost no time in following; that, indeed, was why he chose to settle in the neighborhood. For the lady's family lived by Chalk Hill, not far from Lungewater House, on the other side of the river.

"But then a worse misfortune than all before happened to the count—or so it seemed to him—worse, even, than losing his lands and his properties. The lady would not have him. She did not return his love. And, not long after he came, she married another man.

"The count bore this new disappointment very badly. He was not accustomed to rebuff. He fell into a black gloom of anger and misery. To him it was intolerable that the lady should prefer another man. For this, all suffered in his household, but most especially the boy Stiva, who bore kicks and bad words in silence.

"Even now, the count could not believe that the lady would not very soon regret her mistake. He was not one to give up easily. He spent a large part of his days writing, writing, and rewriting a long, furious poem, asking, adjuring, imploring the lady to reconsider. This took him a whole year. And, on Christmas Eve, he sent the poem to her, by the hand of his servant boy, Stiva.

"Now, as I told you, the River Lunge ran

between the properties of Count Boyanus and the
lady, who now lived with her husband in a house
called Sunwool."

"*Sunwool?*" I said. I would have said more, but the
old man was eager to go on with his story. It was as
if a flood, after long battering against some obstruc-
tion, had finally broken through the impediment and
surged on its way, carrying in its wild rush all the
debris and damaged matter that it had withstood for
so long.

"*Da! Da!*" he said impatiently. "Sunwool. So it
was . . . And the shortest path from one house to the
other ran along the bank of the Lunge River, through
a place called Changewood Gully. And here there is
a spot called the Stride. Here the river becomes very
narrow, drawn in between high, rocky banks (or so
I've been informed). From the top of the cliff you
can hardly see the water, which boils along down
below with furious energy. This narrow race is called
the Stride because, from time to time, there have
been men who were bold enough, some foolhardy
enough, to take the standing leap that will carry a
person from one side to the other. (It is not possible
there to take a run, for the sides are too steep and
rocky.)"

I nodded, and asked quickly, "Did Stiva go that
way when he delivered the poem?"

"No! Stiva did not. The count had ordered him

to deliver the envelope by the speediest route—the count always wanted his orders obeyed at once—but Stiva, though illiterate, was not a fool. He did not choose to risk his life at the dangerous spot when there was a footbridge farther downstream, which would take him over in safety. He was neither tall nor strong—why should he be? His diet, for the most part, was bread and porridge. He went by the longer way, and delivered the envelope and came back to his master."

"Did the lady reply to the poem? The beautiful lady?"

"She did not. She was otherwise occupied. On the next day, Christmas Day, news came that she had been delivered of a baby daughter, who was christened Noelle."

"Noelle?" I said. "Then—"

Brushing my interruption aside, the old gentleman went on, "And when these tidings reached Count Boyanus, they made him even angrier and more miserable. To him, it seemed as if that were a short, scornful reply to his year's poetic outpouring. A slap in the face.

"But, as I have said, he was not a man to give up. He sat down at his desk and began another poem . . ."

At this moment a bus drew up beside us. HATFIELD HANGER said the sign on the front.

"Is this our bus?" asked my companion hopefully.

"No, I am afraid it is not . . ."

"Then I resume. A year went by, during which the count shot, fished the Lunge water, brooded angrily, abused his boy Stiva with hard words and kicks, while toiling at a second poem, even more vehement, more anguished, more urgent and beseeching than the first. He wrote and wrote and he rewrote, he crossed out and amended and replaced one line with another. At last the work was done, and all carefully copied out. (The count could not entrust this part to the boy, for the boy could not write. He had to do it himself.) On Christmas evening Boyanus gave the work to the boy Stiva to deliver. By now, from a little lad of nine or ten, Stiva had become a larger boy of ten or eleven. But he still knew no letters or figures, and very little English. He had no time for learning. He led a sad, lonely life, and longed for his own land. But he did not complain. To whom could he, indeed? He served his master faithfully, and received kicks and curses in return.

"'Take the letter to the lady by the shortest way,' ordered Count Boyanus.

"'Yes, master,' said Stiva. But, as before, he did not cross the Lunge River by the Stride, but chose to go the longer, safer way over the footbridge. And the letter was delivered; but again, the lady did not answer, perhaps because, as on the previous occasion, she was engaged, just then, in childbirth. On the day after Christmas, she bore her second child, another daughter. Named Christina."

This time I did not interrupt.

"And again, Count Boyanus, when he heard of this, was furious, hurt, insulted, and unable to recognize or accept the fact that the lady was indeed happy with her chosen husband, and was not at all interested in the count's suit.

"So he sat down to begin a third poem—"

"Excuse me—" I began.

For another bus had now come slowly into view through the misty, frosty haze of the winter day.

CHISEL WOOD said the sign over the driver's cab.

"Is this our bus?" hopefully asked my fellow traveler.

"Yes, this is the one."

So we climbed onboard and paid our fares, and the old gentleman sat down by me.

"I continue my story," he said. "At the end of the third year, the count had completed his most impassioned poem yet. Written with such great heart-burnings and anguish, with blottings and crossings-out of words inserted or lines deleted, as if the central core of his heart were bursting forth, red-hot, into urgent words. When the boy Stiva brought a glass of tea or vodka or brandy to the count's study, he would, as often as not, be greeted by a book flung at his head, or an inkwell. When the poem was done, he put it into an envelope and gave it to Stiva to deliver.

" 'Take it the shortest way,' he ordered.

"The count was not a patient man. He expected his orders to be obeyed on the instant. If not, his punishments were severe.

" 'Yes, master,' said Stiva, and off he went.

"But on this occasion, the count suddenly decided to follow Stiva. Who knows why? Perhaps there was one line in the poem that did not fully satisfy him, and at the last minute, he wished to alter it—"

"Excuse me, sir," I said, "but this is where we have to get off the bus."

"Ah, so, indeed? I thank you, my young friend."

Rather stiffly, the elderly traveler clambered down from the bus platform and stood looking about him.

We had alighted at a crossroads in the middle of a wooded common. Not far off could be heard the roar of water.

LUNGEWATER said one of the arms of the signpost. HOVEL HANGER said another. CHALK HILL said a third. CHISEL WOOD said the fourth.

It was a gloomy, foggy day. One could not see far in any direction. The birch and thorn trees were white with frost crystals.

"I wish to go to Lungewater House," said my

companion. "Can you tell me which way that would be? Are you familiar with this neighborhood?"

"Yes, sir. It is only a ruin now, you know that?"

And a nasty, dismal, decaying dark spot, too, I thought; not a place to visit on a murky winter afternoon.

"Yes, I know," he said. "But my brother lived there once, and I should like to see it. First, though, I should greatly like to see the Stride. This narrow crossing place. Can you tell me how to get there? And also Sunwool House, where the lady lived?"

"Yes, sir. You can take the path by the river. I will be glad to show you; I am going that way myself."

"I am very much obliged to you," said the old man. And so he accompanied me along the footpath, among the white-frosted trees, and as we walked— slowly enough, for he was rather lame—the noise of rushing water grew louder.

"The weather is very misty in your country," said the old man, looking at the shapes of white vapor that hung and drifted among the trees. "No wonder that you have so many tales of ghosts and specters. I believe there are such stories about the Stride. I have been told that it is an especially haunted spot?"

He was right. And that is why—if the truth be told—I would never have been walking that way by myself.

"Sir—please tell me the end of the story. What

happened to Stiva? And to the count? And why have you come all the way here from Dahoungarie?"

"Ah, well, I will tell you. First you must know that in his third year of lonely living at Lungewater House, Stiva had at last made one friend. This was a local lad, Will Thorne. Will was a foot soldier in the army, but when he was at home on leave, he liked nothing better than to poach for trout in Count Boyanus's fishing water. Stiva had encountered Thorne down by the water one evening and, instead of reporting him, had fallen into talk with him. For, by now, Stiva had acquired a few phrases of halting English. And he was greatly surprised when Will Thorne told him that in England there were no slaves, that no man belongs absolutely to his master, that servants are paid wages, and may give notice. And he was even more amazed when Will promised to write a letter for him and try to see that it was sent to his younger brother. For Stiva had a brother, Matvey, who was only four years old when the count was obliged to flee from his lands. Matvey had been left in the charge of a grandmother, an old washerwoman on the count's estate, probably dead by now. And Will Thorne, as it chanced, was soon to be sent, with his regiment, to a part of eastern Europe not too far from where that estate lay. So Stiva told the name of the village where Count Boyanus had his mansion."

"But, sir, please tell me what happened to Stiva? And to the count?"

"Well. The count, striding along the wooded ridge at the end of his garden, wishful to call Stiva back, observed that the boy was taking the longer route and plainly did not intend to jump across the Stride. So he flew into a rage, made haste after the boy, and struck him a violent blow with the butt of the bird gun he always carried. And he ordered Stiva to leap across the gully."

"So the count must have changed his mind about altering the poem?"

"Perhaps. We shall never know if that was his intention. And poor Stiva, shaking and terrified, made a desperate effort to leap across the Stride. But he failed and fell down into the ravine, and the envelope that he carried fluttered away out of his hand. And Stiva's body was never seen again, for the Lunge water there flows into strange deeps and underground whirlpools, from which no object is ever recovered.

"But Will Thorne, secretly poaching the count's waters farther downstream, saw the whole thing happen, and, by chance, he caught the envelope with the count's poem as it came fluttering down.

"The count did not see that; but he did see a man with a fishing rod. And, still full of rage, he shot the man with his bird gun."

"Did the count kill Will Thorne?"

"No. But he was badly hurt, and crawled back home with great difficulty. And when the count made inquiry and found who had been shot, he had Will sent to jail. And there Will's neglected wound became inflamed and he presently died of it.

"Meanwhile, the lady at Sunwool House, the count's lost love, had a third daughter, a sister for Noelle and Christina."

"What happened to the third poem, the one that Will Thorne had caught?"

"Wait, and I will tell you. But first," said my companion, "are we not very close to the Stride?"

We were, and my heart was beating painfully fast. The sound of rushing water almost deafened us. To our left, the waters of the Lunge River, brown and turgid and foamy from long days of recent rain, swung and surged, rolled and plaited, whirling along broken branches, strips of plank torn from jetties, farm tools, all kinds of wreckage swept down from farther upstream, where there had been floods.

There, where we were, the river could not over-leap its banks, for they were far too high, but its angry voice could be heard below as it poured in a thunderous mass toward the narrowest part of the channel.

"Is this what they call the Stride?" asked my companion. "It is a fearsome place."

"The Stride is a little farther along," I told him. "Where the path becomes very narrow indeed and the right-hand bank is even steeper."

The path was slippery now, too, where spraylike mist in the air had turned to fine ice underfoot.

I wondered if it had been like this when Stiva made his leap.

"It would be kind of you to hold my arm," said my companion. It felt thin and stiff as an old dead stick under the rough cloth. We proceeded with great caution.

"I do not wonder that the ghost of Stiva haunts this place," the old man said, half to himself. "Poor, lonely boy. Despite all his ill-usage he was a faithful servant—I think he will have been ashamed that he failed to deliver that last letter."

But I was not sure about that. Would he have been ashamed? Would he not rather have been angry with his master?

"What became of Count Boyanus?"

"Later that same year he, too, fell into the Stride. Some say he was carrying his own poem, his last, to the lady, but there are many that say that the ghost of Stiva pulled him down. The sad, angry ghost."

I could believe that, especially now, at this twilit hour, in this freezing mist and gloom.

We stood on the lip of the Stride and looked

across the deceptively narrow distance to the rocky path, layered with ice, that ran across the opposite cliff. From where we stood, it was hardly more than a table's width over the water to the other side—but not for all the money in the Bank of England would I have attempted that jump.

And yet, there was something about the atmosphere of the place—an urgency, a wish, a will, that beckoned from below . . .

I shivered with cold, and would have been glad to move on, to get away, but the old man still stood motionless, deep in thought, staring intently at the wavering mist-shapes that formed and re-formed and hung below us in the ravine, at the spidery frost-spangled birch trees cresting the cliffs on either side of the river.

"How comes it that you know all these things, sir?" I asked, trying not to shake visibly with cold and fright. "Who are you?"

"I will tell you in a moment. But first I must try to do my best for that poor, homesick spirit. Hold me firmly, if you please, my friend."

He leaned outward a little and called down: "Stiva! Stiva! Do you hear me? Stiva? Are you there?"

He waited. And the roar of the water answered him.

"Stiva! Listen!"

Then followed a long, sonorous message, uttered

in a foreign language, deep and harsh. A prayer, perhaps, or an incantation. His frail old body shook with passion. After he had come to its end, my companion wiped his eyes, then, after a long, silent pause, turned to me.

"Thank you, my friend. That is all. Now we shall go on."

I waited to ask questions until we had passed the narrowest section of the pathway and were on fairly firm, level ground. Then I said again, "Sir, who are you?"

"Why," said the old gentleman, "my name is Matvey. I am Stiva's younger brother."

"But how—how—how did you ever come to hear the story?"

He said, "The poacher, Will Thorne, who caught the last poem as it fluttered down, put it in his pocket. When he was lying in jail, he carried out his promise to write a letter to Stiva's brother, for he remembered the address of the village that Stiva had told him. But before the letter was sent off, Will Thorne died in jail. His few possessions, with the letter and poem among them, were given back to his old mother, and lay, gathering dust, in the bottom of a basket of patches for twenty years. When she died, the basket passed to her daughter, who put it in an attic. Only by chance, not long ago, did a child, rummaging, pull out the old papers. Will Thorne's letter, containing the poem, was clearly addressed to me. In fact I had grown to manhood and moved many times, but it did, in the end, catch up with me.

"I made inquiries about this region, and was dismayed to hear tales that my brother's ghost still haunts the place. And I think this may be because he had not been able to perform his final task. So I came to do it for him."

"You mean," I said, thunderstruck, "deliver the poem?"

"*Da!* Just so. If it is possible. I have the poem here." He tapped his Norfolk jacket pocket. "I think— after all—I will not trouble to look at Lungewater House. You say it is all in ruins. That would be too sad. But, if you will tell me how I can get from this place to Sunwool House?"

"Sunwool? Certainly," I said. "Of course. Of course! Nothing is easier. I am going there myself, as a matter of fact. We follow the bank and cross the bridge."

We did so. Cozily, under the hill ahead of us, among its sheltered walled gardens, lay Sunwool House, where my aunt, Theodosia, the last survivor of three sisters, still lived. And was waiting for my Christmas visit.

She was a small, elfish old lady, with a soft skin like a crumpled birch leaf and eyes of faded river brown. She received my companion without the least surprise. "Ah, yes . . . the poems from Count Boyanus. Do you know, my mother never opened them? I believe she felt that to do so might bring her bad luck. And she had no intention of risking that. She and my father had led such a very happy life. Yes, here are the two poems . . ."

Having unlocked a rosewood desk, she pulled open an inner drawer and took from it two faded yellow envelopes, exactly matching the one that my companion had given to her.

"I am quite sure that you are right, sir; that poor boy Stiva will be very happy to know that his last task has been faithfully executed. And I daresay that from now on he will stop haunting the river-bank, and that will be a great convenience for all the local poachers."

"But the poems, Great-Aunt Theodosia? Aren't you going to read them?" I demanded.

"Why, no, my dear. I think they are much better left unread. That Count Boyanus—I do not like the sound of him at all. A harsh, violent, self-deceiving man. No, no, I think that my mother's judgment of him was perfectly sound. I think by far the best thing to do with the poems is this."

And my great-aunt Theodosia dropped the three unopened envelopes into her drawing-room fire.

⁊⥾

MORGAN ROEHMAR'S BOYS

Vivian Vande Velde

Ashley rearranged the dead bodies, because there's nothing worse than a messy dead body.

Witches, people can recognize by the cackling laughter; werewolves growl and lunge; and vampires swoop. All of those induce honestly earned alarm. But dead bodies just lie or sit there like so much bloodstained laundry, and if people couldn't tell this was a scene of mass murder and were only startled by the light coming on, what was the point of that?

Ashley centered the pitchfork, which had a tendency to sag, in the chest of the man tied to the chair, and she fluffed the hair of the severed head, making sure the executioner's ax was perfectly straight against the neck of the torso a yard or so away, so that the woman's decapitation looked recent, not like tired, old news.

"Barn ready," she said into the microphone of her headset. She took the time to make sure the hanged man—who had a tendency to rotate at the end of his rope—had his face turned toward the door for best effect. She had as much time as she needed between wagonloads, within reason, for the drivers slowed their tractors by the hedgerow, waiting for her all-clear. This ensured she had the light off before they turned the corner, even though the dim red light, enough for her to set up by, was not likely to be glimpsed from between the orchard's trees. Once she gave the okay, she had about thirty seconds to turn off the light before the tractor would circle around and be facing the barn; but she had another two minutes to settle herself before the tractor, pulling the hay wagon, would actually drive in through the open doors. At that point she would flick on the regular light, which was still dim to maximize spookiness.

She heard Tim's voice through the earpiece: "Okay, now, arms and legs inside the wagon—we don't want any injuries"—the "okay" being his signal that he had heard her and was on his way, the rest of what he said maybe necessary and maybe not for this particular wagonload of customers, but spoken to disguise his acknowledgment of her message.

Ashley lay down on her bale of hay, positioned beneath the murderer with the upraised knife. The hay smelled good but—packed tight—was hard and prickled like crazy. The front of her peasant dress was saturated with theatrical blood, and the customers would assume she was simply another mannequin in this tableau of death, until—just as the wagon passed—she would jump up and fling herself at those riding on the back, screaming madly and making as though to grab them.

She pressed the top button on the remote control that turned off the red set-up light, and took off her headset to hide it behind the bale of hay where the customers wouldn't see it. The attached wire pulled the battery pack out of her pocket before she remembered to remove it, and it clunked to the floor. If she broke yet another one of those things, Nikko would throw a fit. In school he was quiet-never-having-a-contrary-opinion Nikko, and she had been *so* interested in him, even though he was a couple years older. But here he was the "family" part of Cristanis Family Farm, and his father let him run the haunted hayrides pretty much on his own, where he was an ogre—never mind that he didn't wear a costume. Ashley had just turned sixteen, and this was the first year she could work here, along with the seniors and college kids. Nikko might have turned out to be a disappointment, but it would be humiliating to get fired after only one week.

Ashley held the earpiece up to her ear and could

hear the background noise of people squealing on one of the wagons, so she knew it still worked. Those performers who never got close to the customers, like the witches in the grotto, could pull the hair of their wigs over the headphones and wear their wires more securely fastened beneath their costumes, but she—and the ghouls who chased the wagon—had to take theirs off at performance time.

As Ashley lay in the dark, she heard a rumble, which she would have assumed was the sound effects from Gina and Jordan doing their magic cauldron act farther up the trail, but it seemed to come from the wrong direction, more from the west, beyond the orchard.

Not thunder, she hoped. The weather forecast had said there was a possibility of storms, but that wasn't supposed to be till later, after closing. There were few enough days for the haunted hayrides. You couldn't have them in September: that was pushing the season, and nobody was interested—or not enough to make being open worthwhile. And you obviously had to stop after Halloween. It was a shame to lose nights to bad weather.

She had just convinced herself that she had imagined the rumble when it came again. Closer this time. Definitely thunder. She could hear the tractor, too. She thought they'd come in—the thunder wasn't that close, but then, through the open doors, she saw a flicker of lightning. The lightning was diffuse—high up and far away—but she could hear the tractor swing around, even before she picked up the headpiece and heard Nikko announcing, "Tractors, return to the loading area. Tractors, back. We've got weather."

Of course the tractors couldn't be out in the open fields during a thunderstorm—they'd be sitting targets for lightning—but the storm wasn't moving in that fast. Still, Nikko's father was a worrier, and that was one area of the operations Nikko had clear instructions about. Pulling the hay wagons in the cold was okay, even in the rain. But not during a thunderstorm.

Ashley heard Kat, in the Witches' Grotto, ask, "Should we come in?"

"Weather stations," Nikko told them, which meant he was hoping the storm was just skirting the area, so they were supposed to take shelter in the outbuildings but be prepared to start again. Nikko certainly wasn't going to be handing out refunds unless he had to.

Ashley reached for the remote control to get the light on and accidentally pressed the bottom button, the one that controlled both the light and the special effects.

A shuddering moan came from the speaker hidden in the hanged man.

The severed head winked.

The legs of the man tied to the chair jerked while the speaker in his body emitted pathetic sobs, which would eventually subside to whimpers, then a death gurgle—which nine out of ten people on the wagons never heard because they were too busy screaming in terror.

Ashley's knife-wielding murderer shouted, "Die, wench, die!" but only once before she cut the power.

This time she pressed the middle button on the remote control. There was only a single hundred-watt bulb for the whole barn, which provided the perfect balance of light and shadow for the show. It was enough to read a book by, at least for a little while, for those who were serious enough about their homework to bring it on the job with them just in case of unusual delays, but that certainly didn't include Ashley. It was enough light to play on a Game Boy, for anyone who had the foresight to bring one. Ashley lay back down on her bale of hay and did a few stomach crunches, but that got old fast with the tight bodice of her peasant's dress instead of sweats.

There was a flash of lightning, distinct this time, and a roll of thunder only a few seconds later.

Nikko's tinny voice was coming through the headpiece, and Ashley picked it up from the floor and put it back on. He must have asked if everyone was secure, because people were counting off.

"Ashley, in the barn," she acknowledged when it was her turn. She had hoped one or two of the ghouls—Ramon, if she'd had a choice, or even Karl—would have decided to shelter in the barn, but they'd gone to the orchard shed, where there was a supply of cocoa, cider, apples, cheese, and doughnut holes. It's hard to compete for a teenage boy's attention when there's food involved.

"Shouldn't be long," Nikko assured them as Ashley, lying on her side, did vertical leg lifts. "Radar shows one area of disturbance just about directly overhead, but the rest is skimming off to the north. Just hang tight." That, despite the fact that the thunder was moving in much closer. Through the open doors of the barn, Ashley got periodic glimpses of trees and sky as clear—for fractions of a second—as though it were full day.

"One Mississippi," someone counted off, "two—"

The thunder was no longer rumbling, but cracking.

"Hey, Ramon," she heard Dan ask—Dan, who, because he rode Riley as part of his Headless Horseman routine, got to wait out the storm in Cristanis Farm's smaller barn, the one by the house, "how many vampires does it take to change a light bulb?"

Ashley lost the answer to static, which was probably from dropping her headpiece and/or the battery pack once too often. She jiggled the wire that connected them, and by then somebody else was off on a different joke — evidence, if she had needed it, that Dan's joke hadn't led to uncontrollable laughter.

"Here comes the rain," Nikko announced, and in another moment it started, as suddenly as someone turning on the shower, sharp and distinct sounding, like an infinite number of thrown pebbles.

Ashley considered getting up to close the doors, but the rain was beating against the back of the barn, not blowing in.

Lightning flashed.

"One Mis—"

The thunder sounded like a tree breaking in half directly overhead.

"You doing okay, Ashley?" one of the Spagnola sisters asked—she couldn't tell whether it was Hannah or Lily.

"Sure," Ashley said, "nice and dry," thinking, *It couldn't have been one of the guys who asked?*

"Of all the places on this farm to be—" Hannah or Lily started, but Nikko interrupted: "C'mon, girls."

"Just saying," whoever it was finished.

Ashley knew what that was all about: the sign out front might say CRISTANIS FAMILY FARM, but all these years later people still called it "the old Roehmar place." When Nikko's grandfather bought the place in the seventies, after it had sat empty for almost a

decade because of the notoriety of what had happened there, he had the original house torn down—
the house under whose floorboards the bodies of a
half dozen boys and young men had been found when
the original owner's live-in woman friend, after a
lovers' spat, told police about the intermittent smell
that coincided with the disappearance of the high-
school cross-country runner in 1968 and the young
Latino farm worker who had supposedly never shown
up in '69.

Two generations of Cristanises lived in the new
house, built on the other end of the property, and
farmed the land. Two generations of Cristanises found
it harder and harder to make ends meet.

Nikko's father had resisted the haunted hayride
idea, but the success enjoyed by several of the other
farms in the area had eventually persuaded him. He
finally agreed, but had two rules:

—Avoid lawsuits.

—And don't cash in on real tragedy.

He forbade anything hinting at Morgan Roehmar
and his obsession with good-looking boys, which
was why the one dismembered body was a woman
(Anne Boleyn, in case anyone asked), who'd lost her
head to an ax, rather than a chain saw. And there
definitely was no display suggesting a police shootout
on a farmhouse's front porch.

Like anybody who'd lived in the area for any

time at all didn't automatically connect this farm with murder.

And like the edginess of something-really-bad-happened-here wasn't the real reason Cristanis Farm's haunted hayride did better than any other in the area.

And the reason the Spagnola sisters were harassing Ashley was because this barn, built by Nikko's grandfather when he'd still had high hopes for the land, was constructed on the one section of the farm that wasn't given over to the new house or its front lawn, or apple orchard, or crop fields—the spot that had been cleared already, because that was where the original Roehmar house had stood.

"I'm doing fine," Ashley assured one and all through the headpiece.

And she was, too.

Until the light went out.

There must have been a lightning strike that hit something important, causing all the lights in the area to go out: after one startled moment of silence, Ashley could hear the chatter as everyone connected by the headphones whooped, as though this were just another special effect thought up by Nikko.

Another flash of lightning, and Ashley blinked because of the brightness—and in the darkness afterward saw someone framed in the doorway of the barn.

"Ramon?" she called.

No answer.

Could Karl or any of the others be touchy enough to remain silent because she'd guessed wrong?

She reached down to the far side of the hay bale she was lying on and scrabbled for the flashlight the Cristanises provided for walking from one site on the farm to the other. Just as her fingers closed on the flashlight, she felt the tug of the wire that attached headpiece to battery pack. And then she didn't feel it and knew that she'd pulled the wire loose, but that was not her immediate concern.

She pressed the flashlight's switch and swung the light toward the doorway.

Where no one was standing.

She could make out the bales of hay, the farm implements—since, besides the haunted hayrides, this was a real working barn—the posed dummies, the hanged man spinning slowly in the breeze. But there was no one in the doorway.

As there shouldn't be.

Maybe it was some weird afterimage left by the lightning and induced by the Halloween atmosphere on the farm or by thinking of the guys Morgan Roehmar had murdered. Or she'd seen the hanged man and, trick of the shifting light, he'd seemed farther away, in the doorway.

Or maybe whoever it was had stepped away into the darkness outside.

Still sitting on the bale of hay, Ashley flicked the flashlight so the beam hit the battery pack. The wire that should have been stretched out to the head-phones lay limp on the floor.

Aiming the light back at the doorway, she set the flashlight next to her and picked up both pieces of the headset. Glancing up repeatedly to make sure who-ever it was—if there *was* a whoever—couldn't sneak up on her, she tried to thread the jagged end of wire back into what she thought was the appropriate hole of the headphones, but there wasn't even static.

Okay, so there was no calling for help.

If help was needed.

Ashley sincerely hoped her paranoia was in over-drive.

Still, it was no good to try to simply *hope* danger away. If someone was lurking out there, ignoring him was not going to make him go away. She picked up the flashlight and moved to the doorway of the barn. The rain was still beating down, giving the air a fresh, clean smell but making a muddy puddle of the entryway.

No footprints in the mud.

Was the force of the rain enough to wash away footprints in the time—surely no more than thirty seconds—she had delayed to check the headphones?

She shone the flashlight into the darkness out-side, but most of the light bounced off the sheets of rain, not making it to the trees several hundred feet away.

A well-timed bolt of lightning lit up the entire area just as a simultaneous crack of thunder jarred her teeth—and there wasn't a trace of anyone.

Of course, whoever it was—again, if there'd been a whoever—could have circled around to the back of the barn.

But there isn't anyone, Ashley told herself. The tractor drivers kept a count of how many people were in each wagon, because Nikko would have frowned on their losing a customer. Who would be wandering around the farm on such a miserable night? The workers had all sought shelter, the customers were presumably accounted for.

Still, she pulled the barn doors shut, which was only a sensible precaution in case the wind shifted, but she was very aware that the latch and padlock were on the outside because there was never any reason to lock yourself into a barn, only to close it up after you left. On this side there was only a piece of twine fastened to one door. The loop end slipped over a block of wood nailed into the other door— protection against the wind swinging the doors wide open, but hardly security in case someone wanted to get in.

Facing the doors as she fastened the twine, Ashley felt a tingle in the spot between her shoulder blades. A somebody's-behind-you-watching-you sort of feeling. And she realized that the person she'd half convinced herself she hadn't seen in the doorway could have ducked down when she blinked.

And could have gotten back up again while she stood looking in totally the wrong direction.

She whipped around, the beam of her flashlight skittering over Anne Boleyn's head, the hanged man, the man tied to the chair, the knife-wielding man she thought of as her murderer.

Nothing.

She played the light up into the loft. Nikko hadn't put anything up there this year because last year's mannequin hadn't worked well—a man sitting on the edge, holding a gun to his head. When that year's barn attendant would turn the light on, there was a tape recording of a gunshot, and the man fell backward so that only his feet, still dangling over the edge, showed. Or at least that was the theory. Several times he didn't fall far enough, which looked lame. Once he fell forward and off, almost hitting the people in the wagon, not only exposing the mannequin's wires but—Nikko's father supposedly ranted—also exposing the Cristanis Family Farm to a potential lawsuit. So now there were only a couple bats and world-class-size spiders dangling from the edge of the loft.

Were they vibrating more than they should have from the wind and from her closing the doors?

No way, Ashley told herself, could someone have climbed up that ladder in the short time she'd had her back turned.

And she would have heard.

Wouldn't she?

The rain was still hitting the back of the barn with so much force that it almost sounded like hail.

She walked around the downstairs section, circling the mannequins and the bales of hay, shining her flashlight into each gloomy corner.

There was definitely no one down here.

The doors rattled.

But that was just the wind.

She was fairly sure.

She shone the light up into the loft again and weighed her options. It was almost impossible that anybody was up there, but she knew she couldn't remain in this barn without making sure. There was probably nobody outside, either, but that was more plausible than that there was somebody in here. If she left the barn to get away from the person who probably wasn't in the loft, she might run into the person who could be outside. And, outside, she'd face the more real dangers of having a lightning-struck branch fall on her, or of falling herself or twisting her ankle in the slickness underfoot, or of catching pneumonia. And she'd have to explain why she'd left the barn, and the others would know how badly spooked she'd been, and they'd laugh at her and say she was too young to work here after all.

There is, she assured herself, *nobody in the loft.*

She looked around for a weapon. Just in case. The pitchfork in chair-guy's chest, the ax that had severed Anne Boleyn's head, the knife held by the man murdering the wench—all those were plastic. There had to be a real pitchfork somewhere around the barn, but it was put away so nobody could hurt themselves with it.

As she was likely to do—if she could even find it—if she tried climbing the ladder with it.

Ashley wound the wire from the headphones' battery pack around her hand, figuring she could climb with that and, potentially, use it to smack any intruder. She put her foot on the lowest rung of the ladder and realized the flashlight made climbing dangerous. It was too fat: she couldn't hold it *and* get a secure grip on the ladder. What good would she accomplish if she proved to herself she was alone but fell to her death doing so? She tried holding the end of the flashlight in her mouth, but—besides it being gross—she was too likely to gag.

So she set the flashlight down on the floor, pointing it up into the loft so she could see.

Ashley once more set foot to the lowest rung. She took a steadying breath, then climbed all in a rush, hesitating only when the top of her head came even with the floor of the loft.

She gave a quick peek.

Nothing *waiting* for her, anyway.

She scrambled the rest of the way up, then swung the battery pack, just in case anyone came lunging out of one of the corners. But the only thing it made contact with was her own wrist.

See, she chided herself.

Then she *did* see it, a crouched figure in the right-hand corner. The light from the flashlight was too dim for her to make out any details. She swung the battery pack again, and it broke loose from the wire, so that a second later it hit the floor down below with a dull thud. But the shadow didn't approach, or move. Or make a sound.

That gave her the courage to take a step closer.

It was the stupid suicidal dummy from last year, abandoned and shoved into this far corner in disgrace.

Ashley realized how raggedly she had been breathing.

It smelled of dusty heat up here, despite the coolness of the October night, the air thick and hard to breathe.

But she stayed long enough to check behind

the dummy, behind the hay bales—though nothing bigger than a medium-size dog could have hidden behind them. Still. Just to be sure.

She was embarrassed for being as silly as a grade-school kid scaring herself with her own campfire story. Though the storm was moving away, it had brought a cold front in with it. On the other hand, the force of the rain was lessening, and most people would rather see the show even if it was cold and drizzling out. If Nikko was right about no other lightning in the area . . .

But, no, she realized as she climbed back down the ladder: the show couldn't resume until the electricity came back on. Whether it did or the show was canceled, somebody should be noticing soon that they weren't getting any responses from her over the headphones. Nikko would send someone to check on her, and she would have to admit to breaking the headphones. Maybe she could come up with a good explanation before then, an explanation that wouldn't make her sound like a klutz or like a baby spooked by shadows.

She was unwrapping the battery-pack wire from around her fingers as she turned to face the doors to pick up the flashlight. Beyond the circle of light aimed past her at the loft, she saw a figure standing in front of the barn doors, the doors that were still fastened by twine.

Not the hanged man. Definitely not another left-over dummy.

But even as she backed away, she noticed things. Like that he was not a man but a boy about her age, or at the most a year or two older. Which, of course, did not make him any less dangerous. Despite the light from the flashlight shining in her eyes, she could see him clearly enough to make out that his hair was dry, not dripping in his face as it should have been in this downpour.

Then lightning flashed—not that close, but visible through the gap between the barn doors, enough to illuminate where the boy stood.

Except there was no boy.

Then the barn was dark again.

And he was back.

He flung his arm up to protect his eyes and whispered, "Please don't hurt me."

It was a relief, of sorts, that he was afraid of her, except that she knew animals sometimes attacked out of fear. Still, it indicated he hadn't come in here planning on hurting her. Except how could he have gotten in? How could he disappear in lightning that wasn't bright enough to dazzle her eyes?

Ashley darted forward, grabbed the flashlight, and swung the beam in his direction.

He disappeared. Like a movie that fades off the

projection screen when the overhead lights come on, he paled into nothingness.

There was no reasonable explanation for that.

Ashley backed up and tripped over one of the bales of hay, making her sit down hard and fast, her bottom skimming the edge of the bale, which scraped her back on her way down to the floor. The beam of light jerked up and down—over the doors, onto the floor—but she knew to hold tight, and she didn't drop the flashlight.

In the half-moments the light was not shining on him, the boy reappeared, crouching on the floor, his arms over his head as though warding off a blow.

Ashley tasted blood and realized she'd bitten her lip. She watched the shadow cast by the hanged man, creeping over the far wall, over the doors, as he twisted in the air currents, silent except for the creaking of the beam. She was amazed she could hear that little sound over the pounding of her heart.

"Who are you?" Ashley demanded of the boy who was no longer there. "What do you want?"

Thunder grumbled, off in the distance, but the boy didn't answer.

Ashley felt she knew who he had to be, though her rational mind kept trying to push that possibility away.

He was a dead boy, one of Morgan Roehmar's victims. Brought back . . . by what? The electricity of the storm? The particular night? Some alignment of the planets?

By the lack of light, definitely. Ashley kept a firm hold of the flashlight.

Then thought about all the dark corners of the barn behind her.

Still sitting on the floor, she swung the flashlight in an arc around her.

And once more glimpsed the boy by the doors as her beam of light chased the darkness around the barn.

He was gone once she aimed the flashlight directly in front of her again.

So, apparently something confined him to that spot. Good.

She sat with the comforting realness of the bale of hay pressing against her back and tried to keep her teeth from chattering.

C'mon, Nikko, she thought.

Ramon.

Somebody.

Morgan Roehmar had lured boys into trusting him — good-looking boys, the talk went, though of course the original news coverage had been way before her time. And she had never paid attention when, every so often, there would be a retrospective in the newspapers, usually on the anniversary of the day Roehmar had held police at bay for almost twelve hours before a police sharpshooter picked him off from where he'd barricaded himself on his front porch. Even as the coroner carried his dead body out, the dogs the police had brought into the house had gone frantic, finding the two bodies the girlfriend had told the police might be there, but still the dogs wouldn't settle down, till they found another. Then another. Then another. Five bodies all told, or six— Ashley couldn't even remember. It was a story for campfires, for Halloween, for parents to warn their kids with, saying, "Even here, in a quiet place like this . . ."

The boy Ashley had glimpsed had been good-looking, what she'd seen of him before he'd dropped into a defensive crouch.

She tried to remember the details. She remembered the high-school runner, because there was a picture of him still up in the trophy case outside the gym all these years later. This hadn't been him. The migrant worker? He hadn't seemed dark enough, but maybe. She thought there'd been a younger boy, twelve or thirteen, tricked by Roehmar asking for help finding a lost puppy—but that might be confusing two stories into one. And she was drawing a total blank on the other two, or possibly three, guys.

The only face she could truly remember from the papers was Roehmar's—he'd been in his fifties, kind of jowly but clean-shaven, not much hair on top of his head, either, and what was there was gray. Ashley had always thought there was an intrinsically evil look about his eyes, but maybe that came from afterward, from knowing what he did, for he didn't seem to have had trouble fooling people. Somehow or other—and he had different ways for the different boys over the several years and several counties he'd done this—Roehmar tricked his victims into trusting him long enough to overpower them, then he tied them up and strangled them with electrical wire.

No wonder this kid was acting terrified. The last few minutes of his life must have been awful.

Which was no reason for him to hang around frightening her.

But she couldn't get his words out of her head: *Please don't hurt me.*

There'd been nobody to help him then. Could she help him now?

There's nothing I can do, she told herself.

Nothing to save his life, obviously. But why was his spirit—his ghost, whatever (she felt silly even thinking the words to herself)—still here? Something must be wrong.

Well, duh.

Something *beyond* that he'd been killed in a terrible way. All the boys had been killed in a terrible way. Why was this one still here—she cringed again at the thought—haunting?

No matter where Roehmar killed them—and the police suspected it hadn't been at the house—afterward he brought the bodies back to the farm, cut them into manageable pieces, wrapped them in plastic bags, and shoved them into the basement crawl space. Even when the police had come in response to the girlfriend's complaint, they had originally just been going through the motions required to follow up on her accusation—not taking her seriously until Roehmar freaked out.

But he *had* freaked out. And so he had been killed. The bodies had been brought out of their hiding place, identified, buried. Though their murderer had never been brought to trial, he *had* been brought to justice.

Ashley flicked the beam of light away from the doors, revealing the kid once more. He had sat down on the floor, his arms encircling his knees, which were drawn up to his chest. He was rocking back and forth, watching her. Unable to stand it, Ashley aimed the flashlight directly at him again.

She could get a priest, she thought, to come out here and bless the place.

Yeah, right. And she would get the priest out here by telling him what, exactly? *Bless me, Father, for I have seen a ghost . . .*

She turned the flashlight away from him once

more. "What do you want?" she demanded, recognizing that her voice came out harshly.

He *was* good-looking: dark hair, huge dark eyes. He swallowed hard before answering, in a little voice, "I want to go home."

The flashlight shook in Ashley's hand, making the hanged man's shadow dance, but she kept the beam of light away from the area by the doors.

Does he know he's dead? she wondered. She didn't dare ask for fear that such knowledge might make a ghost more powerful, more malevolent. Or was the lack of knowledge precisely what was keeping him here? Ashley just didn't know how all this supernatural stuff worked. So she only repeated, "Home?"

"Don't let him hurt me any more," the kid said.

"He won't," Ashley assured him. "He can't."

At least the kid stopped rocking. "Why didn't they take me?" he asked. "Why did they take the others but not me?"

That sent a chill up her back. "Who are you?"

The boy began rocking again. Though he looked Ashley's age, his fear made him appear much younger. "I can't remember," he cried in desperation. "Everything's fading away from me." He held his hands out to her. "Like with the light."

She could see through him: she could see his torso through his hands, the doors through his torso.

She angled the flashlight's beam farther away from him, and the lack of light made him easier to see.

"At least there were the others before," he said, and Ashley wondered if Roehmar had kept one boy alive longer than the rest, though she had never heard anything like that. But then the boy added, "The ones in the crawl space. But they took them away, and they left me."

"Where are you?" Ashley asked. Dumb question. He was obviously right in front of her in the barn.

But he didn't say that. He said, "Here. Under the porch."

Her breath came in a hiss.

There was another body.

The police had found the plastic bags under the floorboards, crammed into the crawl space. And they'd already found more than they had thought they'd find. But there was another. Buried in the ground. The house had stood empty, then been knocked down; the barn had eventually gone up in the same place—but without a foundation, without digging.

"Can't they come again to get me?" he pleaded. "Can't you show them?"

"Yes," she assured him.

"Will you stay with me until"—she suspected he altered the direction of his question—"until then?"

"Of course." Though it was the last thing in the world she wanted to do.

Nikko, or whoever he sent to check up on her, would come bearing flashlights, but she would make them turn the lights off, and then they would see. She would not be silly, easily spooked Ashley, but Ashley who had solved a mystery, who was helping to lay a spirit to rest.

"Can you call them to come now?" the lost boy asked.

"My headphones are broken," she explained.

"I'm good—I used to be good"—the kid closed his eyes—"with electronic stuff."

She went back to gather the pieces: headphones, loose wire, and battery pack. The thunder was a distant grumble now; she could hear the water dripping off the roof, but no longer the sound of rain battering the barn or the ground. Help would be here soon enough, but she couldn't bear to tell the poor dead kid to wait any longer than he already had. "Can you touch . . ."—Um, *how did one word* THAT?—"solid things?"

"Sometimes," the boy replied from his seat by the doors, so weak and wistful she worried he was about to fade away again. If he did, how would she ever know when he'd come back so she could rescue him?

She rushed to the doors and crouched beside him. He looked more solid than ever, and when she leaned in close, her hand brushed his arm, and she felt it—she *felt* it, though before she'd seen the light pass through him. "How's this?" she asked, holding the headphones in one hand and the battery pack and the loose wire in the other. The flashlight was back where she'd left it, turned away from the door, beyond the hanged man.

"Fine," he said. His hand touched hers—*touched hers*—as he picked up the wire and stretched it out. "Fine," he repeated. Then, moving more quickly than she'd have thought possible, he wrapped the wire around her neck and began to squeeze.

Ashley clawed at his face, but that just made him tighten the wire even more brutally.

"Stupid girl," he hissed into her ear. "I hate stupid, treacherous girls."

He jerked the wire with each word until the room was spinning. She clawed at her own neck, trying to get her fingers beneath the wire to get it away from her throat, but it was cutting into her, cutting off her breath, cutting off her ability to think—except for the one thought over and over, *How can this be? How can this be?*—until there were no thoughts anymore, no breath, no . . .

Morgan Roehmar let the girl's dead body slump against his and felt the excitement that killing always brought. She *was* stupid. Why in the world did she assume a ghost would choose to look the way its body had looked at the moment of death—all bloody or diseased? Or old? He much preferred to take on the form of the way he had looked at seventeen—the age of the boys he'd killed. But that had been a mistake, killing boys, he now knew, thinking of the woman who had betrayed him to the police, thinking of this one.

He was stronger, now that he'd killed her, and he'd get stronger with each additional death. Already he was no longer limited to the area where the porch had been, where he'd died. Though he had no access to a chain saw or to plastic bags, he did have time before people would come with their damn lights, which would scatter him in the air. He laid her out on that bale of hay beneath the mannequin with the knife, with her peasant dress arranged artfully about her, her hands folded just below her bosom, the headphones over her ears, the battery-pack wire entwined around her fingers the way a funeral home placed rosary beads.

Nice and neat.

Ready for her friends to find her.

For there was nothing, Morgan Roehmar thought, worse than a messy dead body.

☙

WATCH AND WAKE

Retold from a story by Lucius Apuleius

M. T. Anderson

At around eight o'clock in the evening, I finally got off the bus at some town. It was the first town in many miles where there were not lines of people waiting around the demon-towers. Throughout the afternoon, I had watched town after town pass, and in each one, there were the gantries, the pits, the symbols drawn by schoolchildren in crayon stapled to the struts. My head bobbed against the bus window. Villages passed, mini-malls, car lots, grocery stores. I drew on the back of my hand with a pen. The people on the bus stopped talking while we went through the places between towns, the dark places marked by forest, broken tarmac, Ski-Doo rentals, and auto-body repair.

I was nearly out of money, and it was going to be another three days' drive home. I did not know what my parents would say when I got there.

The town where I stepped off was small and without much interest. The streets were pretty empty. They had two stoplights. There was a pizza place and a hair place and an old, rusted demon-tower hung with knives; there was a general store that sold big-headed dolls in the window.

I dragged my duffel bag behind me down the steps of the bus. I thanked the driver. He closed the door and drove away.

I needed a B & B. There were some old houses that I could picture being a B & B. I didn't have any money, but I figured, at a B & B, I might be able to talk them into calling my parents and getting my parents to pay for a night somehow over the phone.

My parents would be surprised. It would be nice, maybe. They would find out I was coming home. I had not heard from them for some time.

I stood with my bag in my hand. Some kids were standing outside the pizza place. They didn't look nice, and they didn't look mean. The boys had more acne than I did, and the girls looked like they were going out dancing.

I walked past them. I went in and sat down at a booth. The two guys behind the counter were talking about their home phones. One had a home phone with lots of noise on the line.

"It's like it's fizzing," he said. "Always. It **really** bugs me."

The other one said, "I bet. That could really get on your nerves."

I left my bag on the seat and went up to talk to them. I asked them about places to stay in town.

One said, "Oh, yeah, sure!"

The other guy said, "Good one!"

I stood there, with my arm on the counter. I guess I looked confused or uncomfortable.

"No place," one explained.

"There was one place," said the other, "but it closed. The dish reception there sucked."

"They got nothing," said the other guy.

I did not know what to do.

I ordered an Italian sub with olive oil. Sometimes when they put olive oil on it, it really hits the spot. The guys looked at me. I patted my belly.

Later, my sub came, and I ate it at the table, reading a book for school. I underlined the important passages. I had a highlighter pen.

At around ten, a man came into the pizza place and asked the guys some questions. They yelled over to me that I was in luck.

"Why?" I said. I stood up.

The man looked at me. He walked over. He said, "I'll pay you to watch a corpse for the night."

I half shrugged. I said, "Why?"

He said, "Come with me." He pointed toward the door. I threw away my paper plate and foil, and closed my book and put it in my pack. I followed him outside.

The kids were gone. The night was cold.

"You on your way home?" the man asked. He was striding.

I nodded.

"That's nice," he said.

I said, "I'd like to know where we're walking."

For a while we walked. He asked me, "Do you know what it's like to feel a grief so deep it's like someone is shouting?"

I waited. He waited. Finally, he said, "My best friend's wife asked me to find someone to sit with his corpse through the night. He's . . ." The man clapped once, loud. Then he put his knuckles together as we walked. He asked, "What's your name?"

"My name is Jim," I said.

"Jim. Ha. You have a last name?"

I looked at him. Then I shook my head.

"It's nice to meet you," he said. He shook my hand. We were walking down the street. There were streetlights. In their light, we could see some old oaks and some rubble and Dumpsters.

He said, "We have a problem with witches. It's witches, here. Nothing is growing anymore. Cooked meat always shivers like it's cold now. It shivers right on your plate, and it bleeds when you poke it. Cars don't run well. The sky stinks. All because of them. Here's the thing. The witches eat the faces of the dead. They can take any form. A mouse, a sparrow, an insect, the lowly roach. This wife, my friend's wife, she needs someone to keep watch."

"How do I keep watch?"

"Just sit up," he said. "They won't approach if someone's awake. They come in through dreams."

We were at a low house on a lawn. The motion light came on near the driveway. We went up to the front door. The man knocked.

The dead man's wife answered. She was beautiful, not much older than me. She had on a T-shirt, and had been rubbing her wet eyes with it. Mascara was smeared across her belly.

"Charlie," she said, "you found someone."

"He'll do it," said the man. "He agreed."

"I didn't agree yet," I said.

"Have a good night, Jenn," said Charlie. "You going to be okay?"

"I'll be okay," said Jenn. "My mom is here."

I went into the house. There were people there in the shadows. They fingered key chains. They were spaced around the living room. The television said, "How can you hold me back? This dog is America's heartthrob!"

"Jenn," said a woman. "Jenn, I called the professional mourners. They're going to call back. They want to know how many people for wailing."

"Okay."

"And the loudness."

"Thanks." The wife led me toward the kitchen. She stopped and looked around the living room. "Who has the baby?" she asked, squinting. "Do you have him?"

"Marty has him," said the woman, nodding her head.

A man had the baby, and was whispering to it.

The wife led me through a door.

The husband was on the kitchen table. They had laid out a nice tablecloth under him, and candles at his head and hands and feet. There was a ring of salt around him to stop death from spreading. He was naked, and all of him was pale. His mouth was open, and his tongue was rich and black.

The wife couldn't look at her husband. She kept her face turned in a different way, like against a garbage wind.

I wondered if she had been in high school when they were married.

"I'm sorry," I said.

She scrunched her neck up. She nodded into the garbage wind.

I leaned against the counter. She went to the cupboard and got out some Triscuits.

She said, "We're going to bed soon. We've been up for two days."

"What am I doing?"

"We'll pay you a hundred dollars."

"Do I just sit here?"

"Just, on the chair. Make sure nothing comes in and calls to him or attacks the face."

"What do I do if something comes?"

She shrugged. "Frighten it." She walked over to the door. "The lights are here. They're on a dimmer." She swiveled the dimmer.

"I think I'll leave them full-strength," I said. I could not stand near the body. His eyes were closed, each one covered with a plastic decal of archangels, but I could not stop myself from believing that his hand would move and grab my leg.

"Don't worry," she said. "Just keep watch."

She left.

I pulled out a chair. It was ten-thirty. Eight hours until dawn.

I sat down. I took out my book. I was about to start reading again, when I thought about the placement of the chair. I wanted to see the door and the corpse at once. I did not want a window at my back.

I stood up and looked at the window. There

were no blinds or shades. Outside, it was pitch black.
There were shells lined up on the windowsill. They
were from a fine day at the beach.

I moved the chair so it was against a closet
door. I sat down again and watched the corpse.

My book was open on my lap.

The door slammed open. I jumped.

It was Jenn, in a different T-shirt and some plaid
boxers. "Do you know what helps me sleep?" she
asked. "Celery." She went and got some out of the
fridge. When she stood up with the bag of celery, I
tried to look in the vent of her boxers to see if she
had anything on underneath. I couldn't tell. She
washed the celery.

"We had the necromancer come earlier today,"
she said. "He told us we should take off the head
before nightfall." She rubbed the groove of the celery
with her thumb. She said, "I just couldn't do that.
There's no way. No way in hell." She shut off the
water by knocking the faucet with her wrist.

She told me good night again and left.

I was alone with the corpse.

The kitchen clock ticked.

I looked down toward my book.

Eight hours.

I took out my highlighter pen. I read several
pages, underlining important passages. I looked up
every so often to make sure the candles were still

burning. I was at the foot of the body. Its gray flab was foreshortened.

In the dead, all muscle is flab.

I looked up after a while. There was a light I hadn't noticed earlier.

The refrigerator door was open a little bit. The light was on. The bag of celery was out on the counter.

I couldn't remember whether I had seen Jenn put it away.

I stood up and went to pick up the bag. It hung from my hand. There was a picture of a farmer turkey on it.

The corpse still had its face. The eyes were closed. The mouth was open.

I put the celery back in the crisper.

While I squatted there, rattling the crisper into place, I thought I heard something behind me.

I did not want to turn around. I wanted to remain facing into the fridge.

I forced myself to look over my shoulder.

The corpse lay motionless on the table. Nothing else moved in the kitchen.

I closed the refrigerator door.

Then I opened it, and took out a Coke, and closed it again.

Caffeine.

I drank the Coke leaning against the counter. I calculated whether I was in grabbing distance of the corpse. The question was whether it would lunge before it grabbed.

The man's hair grew in irregular patches. It was uneven across his chest.

To pass the time, I raised up my shirt and looked at my chest in the window, for comparison. I used the window as a mirror. Outside, through my mirror, it was dark. I reached up and touched my own chest. My hair was straggly, but symmetrical. My nipples tickled.

I tucked in my shirt and sat down.

I read several more pages of the book and outlined important passages. I tried to memorize a few. I could not remember them. I tried to say them out loud, softly. They would not stay in my memory, so I stopped.

There was a weasel in the window.

I dropped the book. It fell between my knees. I looked up at the weasel. On the wall clock, I saw it was three.

The weasel looked in at the body. Its eyes were small and black.

I stood up and went to the window. There was nothing to be afraid of. There was glass between me and the weasel. The weasel showed its teeth. I reached out toward it.

It stared just at me, now.

I knocked on the window, and it crouched. It ran.

I was left, looking out the window at the night.

I turned and went back to my seat.

I sat and picked up my book where it had fallen.

I looked for my page. I couldn't find it.

I couldn't remember what I had been reading about.

I fumbled for my highlighter pen.

I turned the book over. It was warm from my flesh.

I was asleep and knew it. Asleep in my seat near the corpse. Hours passed, and I dreamed of something.

I slept.

Something slapped something else, and I was awake.

I grabbed the book. It almost fell on the floor. There was light.

I stood.

"Morning," said Jenn, coming backward into the kitchen with a tray.

I felt a panic. My skin was numb. I looked at the corpse. I wanted it to still have a face.

She took the tray to the sink and put it down.

"How are you?" she said.

The face was fine. Nothing had happened. The sun was out.

"Anything?" she said.

"There was—it was a weasel," I said. "It came to the window."

Jenn nodded. "A witch," she said. "They can be weasels." She turned around and went to the fridge. "I'd like some orange juice," she said. "You want some orange juice?"

"Yeah," I whispered. My throat was dry. There was a bad taste in my mouth.

"You headed somewhere?" she asked.

"My parents'."

"Nice. There wasn't anything besides the weasel, was there?"

"No. Nope."

"Because sometimes they can be a bear. It takes two of them. They're different paws."

"No."

"You don't mess with that. Bears."

She gave me orange juice and made a big omelet. She put some on a plate for me and some on other plates for members of her family. I stayed in the kitchen and ate. The rest ate in the dining room. Her mother and aunt came in and washed the plates. I still sat there. They told me she would be right down with my money. While they washed, they talked quietly about the arrangements for the funeral.

I stood next to the corpse and looked at it carefully. It was fine. Just fine. It was a narrow escape. I wanted to get away from there. I didn't know if they had some way of telling about my sleep.

When Jenn came back, she was dressed. She had a hundred dollars in cash.

"Thanks," she said. "I was worried you'd fall asleep."

I nodded. I folded up the cash.

She looked at me. "But you didn't fall asleep," she said. It was a question.

I shook my head.

She reached out and took my chin in her hand. She stared at me. She took in my features. I blinked. I tried not to react. "You're a good-looking kid," she said. "Don't make the same mistakes I made."

She dropped her hand. I nodded.

"Good luck getting home," she said. "You have to go far?"

"I'm going by bus."

"Which way?"

"West."

"Sucks," she said. "They've seen huge footsteps in the corn."

I left the mourning household. I could not get away fast enough.

I went down the drive and turned left, to go into town.

◆ ◆ ◆

The buses were not running on their regular schedule. I waited for some hours in the center of town. People went into the market to use the ATM.

At around eleven, I heard noise from up the street. It was the professional mourners walking in front of the corpse. They were dressed for business and hitting themselves in the chest with stones. They were not supposed to see the things of this world anymore, so their eyes were x'd out with short strips of electrical tape. They walked the road by memory, as do all who mourn for someone dead.

They yowled and screamed.

Behind them was the corpse, carried on a white sheet that had been filled with flowers by relatives in black.

In front of them all was Jenn, her head down, her hands behind her back. She wore a matching skirt and jacket. She looked like a little girl.

The family followed behind. Tiny boys were in tiny suits. One of the grandmothers carried an antipasto in plastic wrap.

They were headed to the church just up the street. People came out of businesses to watch them pass.

They were almost past us when a car drove up from behind and began honking.

I was lurking near the pay phones. I did not want to talk to Jenn anymore.

The car drove closer to the stragglers and kept

honking. People in the procession turned and shouted at the driver. The driver just honked more. He stopped diagonally in the middle of the road. I heard the crank of the emergency brake.

He got out of the car. His seat belt was still retracting when he began yelling. "You know what's behind that rouge!" he said. "You know I'm right!" He was an older man. "She killed him!" he yelled. "Poison! Would you stop? Stop walking!"

He got in the car again. The car started up, and lurched forward, and pulled around them, and jerked to a stop in front of them. The procession halted. There was nowhere to go. The car was diagonally in the way. The driver got out again. He was still shouting something. Jenn was stopped now, and turned away. She looked sad.

"She killed him," the man said.

I should have stayed behind the phones. Everyone was curious, though. Everyone on the sidewalks was wandering closer. I went with them.

"Charlie and her," said the old man. "With something." He shook his finger. "Something!"

She looked up and saw me. I thought she wanted to ask me a favor.

I stood there for a second. She didn't say a word. There was a big crowd.

I backed away. She closed her eyes.

I went inside the market. I thought that would

be better. I didn't want to see her anymore. It was a
close escape, and I did not want any more questions.

I sat on a plastic crate near the magazines and
read birthday cards. Over the music on the radio, I
could hear shouting. Something was happening outside. I kept reading the cards. Most of them were
either flowers or dentures and greased men in Speedos.

Some kid ran into the market. He said to the girl
at the counter, "His father says she killed him. He's
accusing her."

"Yeah?"

"They're going to raise the dead. To ask him."

"Now?" she said.

"They've got the necromancer."

The girl looked out the window between the
light-up cigarette signs. She called over her shoulder
to me, "You need help with anything, sir?"

I put back the dog card I was reading.

"There's a guy," the kid told me, "who's dead."
He jerked his thumb outside.

I went with them to watch.

It was not a good idea.

The necromancer was dressed in jeans and a stupid sweater. He had these yellow-colored lenses in
his glasses, and he was kneeling by the corpse on the
side of the road. He was sticking little plastic wedges
into the flesh. The wedges were all over the body.

There was a pretty big crowd. Jenn was crying,

and her mother and father, probably, were standing on either side of her. I saw Charlie, too, standing and looking at the dotted line in the middle of the road. He had on a suit. He scratched under his beard.

Everyone could see the dead man in his nudity. I didn't think about it, until I heard one woman whisper to her friend, "God. I'm glad I decided not to date him."

"Could people stand back?" said the necromancer. "One, two, three steps?"

We all moved away. The necromancer started tying the soul back to the body with lengths of black rubber. He twisted knots.

A man next to me asked a woman, "Did you leave Jarv on the phones?"

"No," she said.

"Who's on the phones?"

"I turned on the machine."

"You can't use the machine," he said. "It's eleven-thirty."

The body had started to move. It was clumsy, because the soul was slipping.

Everyone fell silent. The necromancer rose. The corpse was writhing on the sheet, which lay on the grass. The eyes were open.

The dead man looked down at his own body. He held out his fingers. He said, softly, "I'm dead . . . That's it . . ." He sounded surprised.

His father went and embraced him. He knocked something, and the head rocked back. The head was dead again. The tongue came out. The necromancer squatted and adjusted the rubber cinches, sending the father back with a wave.

The corpse sagged, but its eyes were open. "She killed me," said the dead man. "It was in the vinegar."

We looked at Jenn. She didn't move.

"You killed me," he said. "You and Charlie. It was the vinegar, wasn't it?"

"He's lying," she said. "It's not really him."

"It's me," he said.

"It's not him." She scolded the necromancer. "You were paid to get someone to say this. This is someone else."

The dead man said, "You watched while I fell down."

"This isn't him," she said. "I'd recognize him."

"It's him," said the father. "I can tell."

"You lying, cheating bastard," said Jenn to the necromancer. "How much is the old guy paying you?"

"This is him," said the necromancer. "It's a perfect fit."

"Show me," she said. "Show us that it's him. Because it's not."

"It's me," said the dead man. "And I'll prove it by telling you something that no one else living knows."

"Don't bother," she said.

"I'll tell you," said the dead man.

We waited.

And then he turned and looked around. He searched the crowd. And he turned to me. The dead man turned and raised his sloppy arm and waved his hand toward me. He said, "You left this kid to guard me last night. Sitting by my side. He fell asleep."

She looked at me. Everyone looked at me.

I shook my head.

I tried to back up, but there were people there.

The corpse said to Jenn, "You dressed like a weasel, in a weasel's skin. Then you came for me. He stopped you, so you sent him to sleep."

The necromancer rose and looked at me curiously, as if he saw something. He lightly held out his hands to part the crowd, and said, "Come forward."

They were waiting.

I wanted to run, but they were all waiting for me. I couldn't just turn away and run. Everyone was waiting. So I walked forward.

I stood beside the corpse. The necromancer inspected me.

The dead man said to his wife, "You and your

sisters called my name. I heard you saying, 'Jim.
Come to our feast, Jim.'"

"That's my name," I said. "My name is Jim."

"There are a lot of people named Jim," said the
dead man. "I was once one of them. You were
asleep, Jim, and I was dead, and they called my
name. But you got up first. You went with them.
Sleep is like death. They feasted on your face."

"This is—" I said. "I can't believe this."

"They hid what they had done," said the corpse.
"This—"

The necromancer reached up and touched me
gently, like a lover. He pulled off my nose. It was
wax.

"No," he said glumly, "it's true. Look."

I had no nose. It had been eaten.

I stumbled, but there were hands to hold me
upright. The wax nose lay on the tarmac. He reached
up and pressed my cheek. "I'm going home," I said.
"Just leave it all on until I get home. Leave it on . . ."
But he was tearing off my ear and casting it on the
ground. "It will be fine," I said. "I want a face. They
can sew . . . A doctor will help. I'll go to a doctor.
When I get home. When I get home, they'll see me
and—"

But the necromancer was gouging around my
eyes, pulling pieces of my face off, casting them on

the ground, and more and more was wax, and pieces
fell, and I saw my lashes on the dirt, and felt the tug-
ging of rind after rind peeled from my cheeks, my
forehead, my chin, and did not know any longer
who I was, or where I was going, or how I would
ever get home.

FORBIDDEN BRIDES
OF THE
FACELESS SLAVES
IN THE
NAMELESS HOUSE
OF THE
NIGHT OF DREAD DESIRE

Neil Gaiman

I.

Somewhere in the night, someone was writing.

ii.

Her feet scrunched the gravel as she ran wildly up the tree-lined drive. Her heart was pounding in her chest; her lungs felt as if they were bursting, heaving breath after breath of the cold night air. Her eyes fixed on the house ahead, the single light in the top-most room drawing her toward it like a moth to a candle flame. Above her, and away in the deep forest behind the house, night things whooped and skrarked. From the road behind her, she heard something scream, briefly — a small animal that had been the victim of some beast of prey, she hoped, but could not be certain.

She ran as if the legions of hell were close on her heels, and spared not even a glance behind her until she reached the porch of the old mansion. In the moon's pale light, the white pillars seemed skeletal, like the bones of a great beast. She clung to the wooden door frame, gulping air, staring back down the long driveway as if she were waiting for something, and then she rapped on the door — timorously at first and then harder. The rapping echoed through the house. She imagined, from the echo that came back to her, that, far away, someone was knocking on another door, muffled and dead.

"Please!" she called. "If there's someone here — anyone — please let me in. I beseech you. I implore you." Her voice sounded strange to her ears.

The flickering light in the topmost room faded and disappeared, to reappear in successive descending windows. One person, then, with a candle. The light vanished into the depths of the house. She tried to catch her breath. It seemed like an age passed before she heard footsteps on the other side of the door and spied a chink of candlelight through a crack in the ill-fitting door frame.

"Hello?" she said.

The voice, when it spoke, was dry as old bone — a desiccated voice, redolent of crackling parchment and musty grave-hangings. "Who calls?" it said. "Who knocks? Who calls, on this night of all nights?"

The voice gave her no comfort. She looked out at the night that enveloped the house, then pulled herself straight, tossed her raven locks, and said, in a voice that, she hoped, betrayed no fear, "'Tis I, Amelia Earnshawe, recently orphaned and now on my way to take up a position as a governess to the two small children — a boy and a girl — of Lord Falconmere, whose cruel glances I found, during our interview in his London residence, both repellent and fascinating, but whose aquiline face haunts my dreams."

"And what do you do here, then, at this house, on this night of all nights? Falconmere Castle lies a good twenty leagues on from here, on the other side of the moors."

"The coachman — an ill-natured fellow, and a mute, or so he pretended to be, for he formed no words but made his wishes known only by grunts and gobblings — reined in his team a mile or so back down the road, or so I judge, and then he shewed me by gestures that he would go no farther, and that I was to alight. When I did refuse to do

so, he pushed me roughly from the carriage to the
cold earth, then, whipping the poor horses into a
frenzy, he clattered off the way he had come, taking
my several bags and my trunk with him. I called
after him, but he did not return, and it seemed
to me that a deeper darkness stirred in the forest
gloom behind me. I saw the light in your window
and I . . . I . . ." She was able to keep up her pre-
tense of bravery no longer, and she began to sob.

"Your father," came the voice from the other side
of the door. "Would he have been the Honorable
Hubert Earnshawe?"

Amelia choked back her tears. "Yes. Yes, he was."

"And you — you say you are an orphan?"

She thought of her father, of his tweed jacket,
as the maelstrom seized him and whipped him onto
the rocks and away from her forever.

"He died trying to save my mother's life. They
both were drowned."

She heard the dull chunking of a key being
turned in a lock, then twin booms as iron bolts
were drawn back. "Welcome, then, Miss Amelia
Earnshawe. Welcome to your inheritance, in this
house without a name. Aye, welcome — on this
night of all nights." The door opened.

The man held a black tallow candle; its flickering flame illuminated his face from below, giving
it an unearthly and eldritch appearance. He could

have been a jack-o'-lantern, she thought, or a particularly elderly ax-murderer.

He gestured for her to come in.

"Why do you keep saying that?" she asked.

"Why do I keep saying what?"

"On this night of all nights. You've said it three times so far."

He simply stared at her for a moment. Then he beckoned again, with one bone-colored finger. As she entered, he thrust the candle close to her face and stared at her with eyes that were not truly mad but were still far from sane. He seemed to be examining her, and eventually he grunted, and nodded. "This way," was all he said.

She followed him down a long corridor. The candle flame threw fantastic shadows about the two of them, and in its light the grandfather clock and the spindly chairs and table danced and capered. The old man fumbled with his key chain and unlocked a door in the wall, beneath the stairs. A smell came from the darkness beyond, of must and dust and abandonment.

"Where are we going?" she asked.

He nodded, as if he had not understood her. Then he said, "There are some as are what they are. And there are some as aren't what they seem to be. And there are some as only seem to be what they seem to be. Mark my words, and mark them well,

Hubert Earnshawe's daughter. Do you understand me?"

She shook her head. He began to walk, and did
not look back.

She followed the old man down the stairs.

III.

Far away and far along, the young man slammed his
quill down upon the manuscript, spattering sepia ink
across the ream of paper and the polished table.

"It's no good," he said despondently. He dabbed
with a delicate forefinger at a circle of ink he had just
made on the table, smearing the teak a darker brown;
then, unthinking, he rubbed the finger against the
bridge of his nose. It left a dark smudge.

"No, sir?" The butler had entered almost
soundlessly.

"It's happening again, Toombes. Humor creeps
in. Self-parody whispers at the edges of things. I find
myself guying literary convention and sending up
both myself and the whole scrivening profession."

The butler gazed unblinking at his young master. "I believe humor is very highly thought of in
certain circles, sir."

The young man rested his head in his hands, rubbing his forehead pensively with his fingertips. He sighed. "That's not the point, Toombes. I'm trying to create a slice of life here, an accurate representation of the world as it is, and of the human condition. Instead, I find myself indulging, as I write, in schoolboy parody of the foibles of my fellows. I make little jokes." He had smeared ink all over his face. "Very little."

From the forbidden room at the top of the house an eerie, ululating cry rang out and echoed through the house. The young man sighed. "You had better feed Aunt Agatha, Toombes."

"Very good, sir."

The young man picked up the quill pen and idly scratched his ear with the tip.

Behind him, in a bad light, hung the portrait of his great-great-grandfather. The painted eyes had been cut out most carefully, long ago, and now real eyes stared out of the canvas face, looking down at the writer. The eyes glinted a tawny gold. If the young man had turned around and remarked upon them, he might have thought them the golden eyes of some great cat or of some misshapen bird of prey, were such a thing possible. These were not eyes that belonged in any human head. But the young man did not turn. Instead, oblivious, he reached for a new sheet of paper, dipped his quill into the glass inkwell, and commenced to write.

iv.

"Aye . . ." said the old man, putting the black tallow candle down on the silent harmonium. "He is our master, and we are his slaves, though we pretend to ourselves that it is not so. But when the time is right, then he demands what he craves, and it is our duty and our compulsion to provide him with . . ." He shuddered and drew a breath. Then he said only, "With what he needs."

The bat-wing curtains shook and fluttered in the glassless casement as the storm drew closer. Amelia clutched the lace handkerchief to her breast, her father's monogram upward. "And the gate?" she asked in a whisper.

"It was locked in your ancestor's time, and he charged, before he vanished, that it should always remain so. But there are still tunnels, folks do say, that link the old crypt with the burial grounds."

"And Sir Frederick's first wife . . . ?"

The old man shook his head sadly. "Hopelessly insane, and but a mediocre harpsichord player. He put it about that she was dead, and perhaps some believed him."

She repeated his last four words to herself. Then she looked up at him, a new resolve in her eyes.

"And for myself? Now I have learned why I am here, what do you advise me to do?"

He peered around the empty hall. Then he said, urgently, "Fly from here, Miss Earnshawe. Fly while there is still time. Fly for your life, fly for your immortal aagh."

"My what?" she asked, but even before the words escaped her crimson lips the old man had crumpled to the floor. A silver crossbow quarrel protruded from the back of his head.

"He is dead," she said, in shocked wonderment.

"Aye," affirmed a cruel voice from the far end of the hall. "But he was dead before this day, girl. And I do think that he has been dead a monstrous long time."

Under her astonished gaze, the body began to putresce. The flesh dripped and rotted and liquefied, the revealed bones crumbled and oozed, until there was nothing but a stinking mass of fetor where once there had been a man.

Amelia squatted beside it, then dipped her

fingertip into the noxious stuff. She licked her
finger, and she made a face. "You would appear to
be right, sir, whoever you are," she said. "I would
estimate that he has been dead for the better part of
a hundred years."

V.

"I am endeavoring," said the young man to the
chambermaid, "to write a novel that reflects life
as it is, mirrors it down to the finest degree. Yet as
I write, it turns to dross and gross mockery. What
should I do? Eh, Ethel? What should I do?"

"I'm sure I don't know, sir," said the chambermaid, who was pretty and young and had come to
the great house in mysterious circumstances several
weeks earlier. She gave the bellows several more
squeezes, making the heart of the fire glow an
orange-white. "Will that be all?"

"Yes. No. Yes," he said. "You may go, Ethel."

The girl picked up the now-empty coal scuttle
and walked at a steady pace across the drawing room.

The young man made no move to return to his
writing desk; instead he stood in thought by the fireplace, staring at the human skull on the mantel, at
the twin crossed swords that hung above it upon the

wall. The fire crackled and spat as a lump of coal broke in half.

Footsteps, close behind him. The young man turned. "You?"

The man facing him was almost his double—the white streak in the auburn hair proclaimed them of the same blood, if any proof were needed. The stranger's eyes were dark and wild, his mouth petulant yet oddly firm.

"Yes—I! I, your elder brother, whom you thought dead these many years. But I am not dead—or perhaps, I am no longer dead—and I have come back—aye, come back from ways that are best left untraveled—to claim what is truly mine."

The young man's eyebrows raised. "I see. Well, obviously all this is yours—if you can prove that you are who you say you are."

"Proof? I need no proof. I claim birthright, and blood right—and death right!" So saying, he pulled both the swords down from above the fireplace and passed one, hilt first, to his younger brother. "Now guard you, my brother—and may the best man win."

Steel flashed in the firelight and kissed and clashed and kissed again in an intricate dance of thrust and parry. At times it seemed no more than a dainty minuet, or a courtly and deliberate ritual, while at other times it seemed pure savagery, a wildness that moved faster than the eye could easily follow.

Around and around the room they went, and up the steps to the mezzanine, and down the steps to the main hall. They swung from drapes and from chandeliers. They leaped up on tables and down again.

The older brother obviously was more experienced and, perhaps, was a better swordsman, but the younger man was fresher and he fought like a man possessed, forcing his opponent back and back and back to the roaring fire itself. The older brother reached out with his left hand and grasped the poker. He swung it wildly at the younger, who ducked and, in one elegant motion, ran his brother through.

"I am done for. I am a dead man."

The younger brother nodded his ink-stained face.

"Perhaps it is better this way. Truly, I did not want the house or the lands. All I wanted, I think, was peace." He lay there, bleeding crimson onto the gray flagstone. "Brother? Take my hand."

The young man knelt and clasped a hand that already, it seemed to him, was becoming cold.

"Before I go into that night that none can follow, there are things I must tell you. Firstly, with my death, I truly believe the curse is lifted from our line. The second . . ." His breath now came in a bubbling wheeze, and he was having difficulty speaking. "The second . . . is . . . the . . . the thing in the abyss . . . Beware the cellars . . . The rats . . . the—it *follows!*"

And with this his head lolled on the stone, and his eyes rolled back and saw nothing, ever again.

Outside the house, the raven cawed thrice. Inside, strange music had begun to skirl up from the crypt, signifying that, for some, the wake had already started.

The younger brother, once more, he hoped, the rightful possessor of his title, picked up a bell and rang for a servant. Toombes the butler was there in the doorway before the last ring had died away.

"Remove this," said the young man. "But treat it well. He died to redeem himself. Perhaps to redeem us both."

Toombes said nothing, merely nodded to show that he had understood.

The young man walked out of the drawing room. He entered the hall of mirrors—a hall from which all the mirrors had carefully been removed, leaving irregularly shaped patches on the paneled walls, and, believing himself alone, he began to muse aloud.

"This is precisely what I was talking about," he said. "Had such a thing happened in one of my tales—and such things happen all the time—I would have felt myself constrained to guy it unmercifully." He slammed a fist against a wall, where once a hexagonal mirror had hung. "What is wrong with me? Wherefore this flaw?"

Strange scuttling things gibbered and cheetled in

the black drapes at the end of the room and high in the gloomy oak beams and behind the wainscoting, but they made no answer. He had expected none.

He walked up the grand staircase and along a darkened hall to enter his study. Someone, he suspected, had been tampering with his papers. He suspected that he would find out who later that evening, after the Gathering.

He sat down at his desk, dipped his quill pen once more, and continued to write.

vi.

Outside the room the ghoul lords howled with frustration and hunger, and they threw themselves against the door in their ravenous fury, but the locks were stout, and Amelia had every hope that they would hold.

What had the woodcutter said to her? His words came back to her then, in her time of need, as if he were standing close to her, his manly frame mere inches from her feminine curves, the very scent of his honest laboring body surrounding her like the headiest perfume, and she heard his words as if he were, that moment, whispering them in her ear. "I was not always in the state you see me in now, lassie," he had told her. "Once I had another name and a destiny unconnected to the hewing of cords of firewood from fallen trees. But know you this — in the escritoire, there is a secret compartment, or so my great-uncle claimed, when he was in his cups . . ."

The escritoire! Of course!

She rushed to the old writing desk. At first she could find no trace of a secret compartment. She pulled out the drawers, one after another, and then perceived that one of them was much shorter than the rest, upon which she forced her white hand into the space where the drawer had been and found, at the back, a button. Frantically, she pressed it. Something opened, and she put her hand on a tightly rolled paper scroll.

Amelia withdrew her hand. The scroll was tied with a dusty black ribbon, and with fumbling fingers she untied the knot and opened the paper. Then she read, trying to make sense of the antiquated handwriting, of the ancient words. As she did so, a ghastly pallor suffused her handsome face, and even her violet eyes seemed clouded and distracted.

The knockings and the scratchings redoubled. In but a short time they would burst through, she had no doubt. No door could hold them forever. They would burst through, and she would be their prey. Unless, unless . . .

"Stop!" she called, her voice trembling. "I abjure you, every one of you, and thee most of all, oh, Prince of Carrion. In the name of the ancient compact between thy people and mine."

The sounds stopped. It seemed to the girl that there was shock in that silence. Finally, a cracked voice said, "The compact?" and a dozen voices, as ghastly again, whispered, "The compact," in a susurrus of unearthly sound.

"Aye!" called Amelia Earnshawe, her voice no longer unsteady. "The compact."

For the scroll, the long-hidden scroll, had been the compact — the dread agreement between the lords of the house and the denizens of the crypt in ages past. It had described and enumerated the nightmarish rituals that had chained them one to another over the centuries — rituals of blood, and of salt, and more.

"If you have read the compact," said a deep voice from beyond the door, "then you know what we need, Hubert Earnshawe's daughter."

"Brides," she said simply.

"The brides!" came the whisper from beyond the door, and it redoubled and resounded until it seemed to her that the very house itself throbbed and echoed to the beat of those words — two syllables invested with longing, and with love, and with hunger.

Amelia bit her lip. "Aye. The brides. I will bring thee brides. I shall bring brides for all."

She spoke quietly, but they heard her, for there was only silence, a deep and velvet silence, on the other side of the door.

And then one ghoul voice hissed, "Yes, and do you think we could get her to throw in a side order of those little bread-roll things?"

VII.

Hot tears stung the young man's eyes. He pushed the papers from him and flung the quill pen across the room. It spattered its inky load over the bust of his great-great-great-grandfather, the brown ink soiling the patient white marble. The occupant of the bust, a large and mournful raven, startled, nearly fell off, and only kept its place by dint of flapping its wings several times. It turned, then, in an awkward step and hop, to stare with one black bead eye at the young man.

"Oh, this is intolerable!" exclaimed the young man. He was pale and trembling. "I cannot do it, and I shall never do it. I swear now, by . . ." And he hesitated, casting his mind around for a suitable curse from the extensive family archives.

The raven looked unimpressed. "Before you start cursing, and probably dragging peacefully dead and respectable ancestors back from their well-earned graves, just answer me one question." The voice of the bird was like stone striking against stone.

The young man said nothing at first. It is not unknown for ravens to talk, but this one had not done so before, and he had not been expecting it to. "Certainly. Ask your question."

The raven tipped its head to one side. "Do you like writing that stuff?"

"Like?"

"That 'life as it is' stuff you do. I've looked over your shoulder sometimes. I've even read a little here and there. Do you enjoy writing it?"

The young man looked down at the bird. "It's literature," he explained, as if to a child. "Real literature. Real life. The real world. It's an artist's job to show people the world they live in. We hold up mirrors."

Outside the room, lightning clove the sky. The young man glanced out of the window: a jagged streak of blinding fire created warped and ominous silhouettes from the bony trees and the ruined abbey on the hill.

The raven cleared its throat.

"I said, do you enjoy it?"

The young man looked at the bird, then he looked away and, wordlessly, he shook his head.

"That's why you keep trying to pull it apart," said the bird. "It's not the satirist in you that makes you lampoon the commonplace and the humdrum. Merely boredom with the way things are. D'you see?" It paused to preen a stray wing feather back into place with its beak. Then it looked up at him once more. "Have you ever thought of writing fantasy?" it asked.

The young man laughed. "Fantasy? Listen, I write literature. Fantasy isn't life. Esoteric dreams, written by a minority for a minority, it's—"

"What you'd be writing if you knew what was good for you."

"I'm a classicist," said the young man. He reached out his hand to a shelf of the classics—The Mysteries of Udolpho, The Castle of Otranto, The Saragossa Manuscript, The Monk, and the rest of them. "It's literature."

"Nevermore," said the raven. It was the last word the young man ever heard it speak. It hopped from the bust, spread its wings, and glided out of the study door into the waiting darkness.

The young man shivered. He rolled the stock themes of fantasy over in his mind: cars and stockbrokers and commuters, housewives and police, agony columns and commercials for soap, income tax and cheap restaurants, magazines and credit cards and streetlights and computers . . .

"It is escapism, true," he said aloud. "But is not

the highest impulse in mankind the urge toward freedom, the drive to escape?"

The young man returned to his desk. He gathered the pages of his unfinished novel and dropped them, unceremoniously, in the bottom drawer, amongst the yellowing maps and cryptic testaments and the documents signed in blood. The dust, disturbed, made him cough.

He took up a fresh quill and sliced at its tip with his penknife. In five deft strokes and cuts, he had a pen. He dipped the tip of it into the glass inkwell. Once more he began to write:

viii.

Amelia Earnshawe placed the slices of whole-wheat bread into the toaster and pushed it down. She set the timer to dark brown, just as George liked it. Amelia preferred her toast barely singed. She liked white bread, as well, even if it didn't have the vitamins. She hadn't eaten white bread for a decade now.

At the breakfast table, George read his paper. He did not look up. He never looked up.

I hate him, she thought, and simply putting the emotion into words surprised her. She said it again in her head. *I hate him.* It was like a song. *I hate him for his toast, and for his bald head, and for the way he chases the office crumpet — girls barely out of school who laugh at him behind his back, and for the way he ignores me whenever he doesn't want to be bothered with me, and for the way he says, "What, love?" when I ask him a simple question, as if he's long ago forgotten my name. As if he's forgotten that I even have a name.*

"Scrambled or boiled?" she said aloud.

"What, love?"

George Earnshawe regarded his wife with fond affection, and would have found her hatred of him astonishing. He thought of her in the same way, and with the same emotions, that he thought of anything that had been in the house for ten years and still worked well. The television, for example. Or the lawn mower. He thought it was love.

"You know, *we* ought to go on one of those marches," he said, tapping the newspaper's editorial. "Show we're committed. Eh, love?"

The toaster made a noise to show that it was done. Only one dark brown slice had popped up. She took a knife and fished out the torn second slice with it. The toaster had been a wedding present from her uncle John. Soon she'd have to buy another, or start cooking toast under the grill, the way her mother had done.

"George? Do you want your eggs scrambled

or boiled?" she asked very quietly, and there was something in her voice that made him look up.

"Any way you like it, love," he said amiably, and could not for the life of him, as he told everyone in the office later that morning, understand why she simply stood there holding her slice of toast, or why she started to cry.

IX.

The quill pen went *scritch scritch* across the paper, and the young man was engrossed in what he was doing. His face was strangely content, and a smile flickered between his eyes and his lips.

He was rapt.

Things scratched and scuttled in the wainscoting, but he hardly heard them.

High in her attic room, Aunt Agatha howled and yowled and rattled her chains. A weird cachinnation came from the ruined abbey: it rent the night air, ascending into a peal of manic glee. In the dark woods beyond the great house, shapeless figures shuffled and loped, and raven-locked young women fled from them in fear.

"Swear!" said Toombes the butler, down in the butler's pantry, to the brave girl who was passing herself off as chambermaid. "Swear to me, Ethel, on your life, that you'll never reveal a word of what I tell you to a living soul . . ."

There were faces at the windows and words written in blood; deep in the crypt a lonely ghoul crunched on something that might once have been alive; forked lightning slashed the ebony night; the faceless were walking; all was right with the world.

THE DEAD
AND THE
MOONSTRUCK

Caitlín R. Kiernan

Beneath Providence, below the ancient yellow house on Benefit Street where silver-eyed vampires sleep away the days and pass their dusty, waxwork evenings with Spanish absinthe and stale memories; this house that once belonged to witches, long ago, this house with as many ghosts and secrets and curses as it has spiders and silverfish—beneath the yellow house, at half past midnight on a bitter February night, Mesdames Terpsichore and Mnemosyne are finishing a lecture with corporeal demonstrations. Lessons for ghoul pups and for the children of The Cuckoo—the changeling brats stolen as babies and raised in the warrens—and for an hour the two old hounds have droned on and on and on about the most efficacious methods for purging a corpse of embalming fluid and other funereal preservatives before it can be safely prepared in the kitchens. The skinny, mouse-haired girl named Starling Jane nodded off twice during the lecture, earning a snarl from Madam Mnemosyne and a mean glare from Madam Terpsichore's blazing yellow eyes.

"That's all for tonight," Madam Terpsichore growls, folding shut the leather satchel that holds her scalpels and syringes, her needles and knives. "But every one of you'd best know *all* the purgatives and detoxicants by the morrow. And you, young lady"— and now the *ghul* points a long and crooked finger at Starling Jane, one ebony claw aimed straight at her heart—"*you* need to learn that the day, not the classroom, is the proper place for sleeping."

"Yes, ma'am," Starling Jane whispers, and keeps her eyes on the dirt floor of the basement, on her bare feet and an ivory scrap of bone protruding from the earth. "It won't happen again."

There's a hushed titter of laughter and guttural yapping from the rest of the class, and Jane pretends that she's only a beetle or a small red worm, something unimportant that can scurry or slither quickly away, something that can tuck itself out of sight in an unnoticed cranny or crevice, and she'll never have to sit through another dissection lecture or be scolded for dozing off again. Madam Mnemosyne silences the muttering class with a glance, but Jane can still feel their eyes on her, and "I'm sorry," she says.

"I should think that you are," Madam Terpsichore barks. "You're plenty old enough to know better, child," and then, to the other students sitting cross-legged on the basement floor, "Mistress Jane's Third Confirmation is scheduled for the full Hunger Moon, four nights hence. But perhaps she isn't ready, hmmmm? Perhaps she'll be found wanting and the razor jaws will close tight about her hands. Then maybe we'll have her meat on the slab before much longer."

"And no nasty embalming fluid to contend with," Madam Mnemosyne adds.

"Ah, she would be sweet," Madam Terpsichore agrees.

"I'm sorry," Jane says again. "But I'll be ready on the moon."

Madam Terpsichore flares her wide black nostrils, sniffs at the musty cellar air, and her eyes glitter in the candlelight. "See that you are, child," she says. "It would be a shame to lose another sprout so very soon after young Master Lockheart's unfortunate rejection," and then she dismisses the class, and Jane follows all the others from the basement into the old tunnels winding like empty veins beneath the city.

Later, after Elementary Thaumaturgy and Intermediate Necromancy and a rambling, unscheduled address on the history of the upper nightlands by Master Tantalus, visiting Providence from the Boston warrens. After dinner and the predawn free hour, after all the time lying awake in her narrow bunk, wishing she were asleep but afraid to close her eyes, Starling Jane finally drifts out and down, slipping through the familiar dormitory smells of wet masonry and mildew and millipedes, past the snores and grunts and gentle breathing noises of those who aren't afraid of their dreams. A hundred feet beneath the day-washed pavement of Angell Street, and she spirals easily through velvet folds of consciousness and unconsciousness. Countless bits of senseless, inconsequential remembrance and fancy—simple dreams—leading and misleading her step by step, moment by moment, to the nightmare place she's visited almost every morning or afternoon for two months.

That place where there is a wide blue sky, and the sun hanging inconceivably bright directly overhead, where there is grass and the scent of flowers, and she stands at the top of a hill looking down on a sparkling sea.

"You should have stayed with me," her mother says from somewhere close behind her, and Jane doesn't turn around, because she doesn't want to see. "If you'd have stayed with me, I'd have loved you and you'd have grown up to be a beautiful woman."

The salt-warm wind off the sea makes waves in the tall grass and whistles past Starling Jane's ears.

"I would have stayed," she says, just like she always says. "If they'd have let me. I would have stayed if I'd had a choice."

"I knew I'd lose you," her mother replies. "Before you were even born, I knew the monsters would come and steal you away from me. I knew they'd hide you from me and make you forget my face."

"How could you have known all that?" Jane asks. Down on the beach, there are children playing with a big yellow-brown dog. They throw pieces of driftwood, and the dog runs after them and sometimes it brings them back again.

"Oh, I knew, all right," her mother says. "Trust me, I knew what was coming. I heard them in the night, outside my bedroom window, scratching at the glass, wanting in."

"I have to pass one more test, Mother. I have to pass one more test and they'll let me live."

"You would have been such a beautiful girl. Just look at what they've made of you instead."

On the beach, the children chase the yellow-brown dog through the surf, laughing and splashing so loudly that Starling Jane can hear them all the way at the top of the hill.

"They'll make you a monster, too," her mother says.

"I wish they could," Jane mutters to herself, because she knows it doesn't matter whether or not her mother hears the things she's saying. "I wish to all the dark gods that they could make me like them. But that's not what happens. That's not what happens at all."

"You could come home. Every night, I sit up, waiting for you to come back, for them to bring you back to me."

"You shouldn't do that," Jane whispers, and the hill rumbles softly beneath her. Down on the beach, the children stop playing and turn towards her. She waves to them, but they don't seem to see her.

Or they're afraid of me, she thinks.

"If you fail the test, they might bring you back to me," her mother says hopefully.

"If I fail, they'll kill me," Jane replies. "They'll kill me and eat me. No one ever goes back, once they're chosen by The Cuckoo. No one."

"But you would have been such a beautiful girl," her mother says again. "I would have given you everything."

"It's the last test," Jane whispers.

Beneath her, the hill rumbles again and the sea has turned to blood and there are wriggling white things falling from the sky. On the beach, the children and the yellow-brown dog have vanished.

"I'll be waiting," her mother says.

And Jane opens her eyes, tumbling breathlessly back into flesh and bone, and she lies awake until sunset, listening to her heart and the sounds the sleepers make and the faraway din of traffic up on Angell Street.

"You're scared," the ghoul pup named Sorrow says, not asking her but telling her, and then he scratches determinedly at his left ear.

"I'm not scared," Starling Jane tells him, and shakes her head, but she knows it's a lie and, worse still, knows, too, that *he* knows it's a lie.

"Sure, and neither was Lockheart."

"Lockheart wasn't ready. Everyone knew he wasn't ready."

They're sitting on stools near one of the tall kitchen hearths, scrubbing tin plates clean with wire-bristle brushes, sudsy water up to their elbows and puddled on the cobbles at their feet. The washtub between them smells like soap and grease.

"Would *you* eat me?" she asks Sorrow. And he grunts and drops the plate he was scrubbing back into the washtub, then tugs thoughtfully at the coarse, straw-colored tuft of hair sprouting from the under-side of his muzzle.

"That's not a fair question. You know under-lings never get delicacies like that. Not a scrap. You'd be served to Master Danaüs and the—"

"I was speaking hypothetically," Jane says, and adds another plate to the stack drying in front of the fire. "If they made an exception and you had the opportunity, would you eat me?"

Sorrow stares at her for a long moment, furrows his brow uncertainly and blinks his yellow eyes, and "Wouldn't you *want* me to?" he asks her finally.

"It wouldn't bother you, eating your best friend?"

Sorrow pulls another plate from the washtub and frowns, looking down at the dishwater now instead of Starling Jane. He scrubs halfheartedly at the bits of meat and gravy and potatoes clinging to the dented tin and then drops the plate back into the tub.

"That wasn't clean, and you know it."

"It's just not a fair question, Jane. Of *course* I'd eat you. I mean, speaking hypothetically and all. I'm not saying I wouldn't *miss* you, but—"

"You'd eat me anyway."

"It'd be awful. I'd probably cry the whole time."

"I'm sure you would," Starling Jane says with a sigh, pulling the plate Sorrow didn't wash out of the tub again. There's a piece of burnt potato skin big as her thumb stuck to it. "I hope I'd give you indigestion. You'd have it coming."

"You really are scared." Sorrow scowls and spits into the washtub.

"You're a disgusting pig, you know that?"

"Oink," Sorrow oinks, and wrinkles his nostrils.

"I'm not scared," Jane says again, because she needs to hear the words. "There's no reason for me to be scared. I've made it past the Harvest Moon and the full Frost Moon. I know my lessons—"

"Book lessons don't get you past the moons. You know that, Jane. Nobody's ever been confirmed because they got good marks."

"It doesn't hurt."

"It doesn't help, either."

"But it doesn't hurt," Jane snarls at him, and flings her wire-bristle brush at his head. Sorrow ducks, and it hits the wall behind him and clatters to the floor.

"You're crazy," Sorrow says, and then hops off his stool, knocking it over in the process. "I might be a pig, but you're crazy."

"You want me to fail. You want me to fail so you can go through all my things and take whatever you want."

"You don't have anything I want," Sorrow barks defensively, and takes a quick step backwards, putting more distance between himself and Starling Jane.

"Yes, I do. That owl skull The Bailiff brought me from Salem. You want that. You've told me more than once that you wish he'd given it to you instead of me."

"I just said I liked it, that's all."

"And that Narragansett Indian arrowhead I found in the tunnels last summer, you want that, too, don't you?"

"Jane, stop and listen to yourself," Sorrow pleads, and takes another step or two away from the hearth. "I do not want you to fail your Confirmation and die, just so I can have your things. That's crazy. You're my friend. And I don't have a lot of friends."

"Friends don't eat each other!"

"Someone's gonna hear you," Sorrow hisses, and holds a long finger up to his thin black lips. "If old Melpomene finds out you're making such a racket, we'll both be scrubbing pots and plates from now till Judgment Day," and he glances nervously over a shoulder into the shadows waiting just beyond the firelight's reach.

"So maybe I don't care anymore!" Jane shouts at him, and then she reaches into the washtub and yanks out a particularly filthy plate. "I'd rather spend the rest of my life washing dishes for that old bat than wind up in her stew pot or roasting on her spit with a turnip stuffed in my mouth!"

"You're not going to fail," Sorrow says, glancing

over his left shoulder again. "You're not going to fail, and no one's going to eat you."

"You don't know that."

"Sure I do."

"Go away. Leave me alone," Jane says, letting the filthy plate slip from her fingers. Soapy, luke-warm dishwater splashes out onto her patchwork apron. "That's all I want, Sorrow. I want to be alone. I think I'm going to cry and I don't want anyone to see. I especially don't want you to see."

"You sure?" Sorrow asks. "Maybe I should stay," and he sits down on the floor as if she's just agreed with him when she hasn't. "I don't mind if you cry."

"Lockheart wasn't ready," she whispers. "That's the difference. He wasn't ready, and I am."

"You bet. I've never seen anyone so ready for anything in my whole life."

"Liar," Jane says, and glares at him. In the hearth, one of the logs cracks and shifts, and, for a moment, the fire flares so brightly that Sorrow has to squint until it settles down again.

"I wouldn't eat you," he tells her. "Not even if they stewed both your kidneys in crab apples and carrots and parsnips and served them to me with mint jelly, I wouldn't eat you. I swear."

"Thank you," Jane replies, and she tries to smile, but it comes out more of a grimace than a smile. "I wouldn't eat you, either."

"Are you going to throw anything else at me?"

"No," she says. "I'm not going to throw anything else at you. Not ever," and she gets up and retrieves her brush from the floor behind Sorrow's stool.

In a life filled past bursting with mysteries—a life where the mysterious and the arcane, the cryptic and the magical, are the rule, not the exception—if anyone were to ever ask Starling Jane what one thing she found the most mysterious, she would probably say The Bailiff. If he has a name, she's never heard it, this very large, good-natured man with his shiny, bald head and full gray beard, his pudgy link-sausage fingers and his rusty iron loop of keys always jangling on his wide belt. Not a vampire nor a ghoul nor any of the other night races, just a man, and Jane's heard rumors that he's a child of The Cuckoo, too, a changeling but something more than a changeling. And there are other rumors—that he's an exiled demon, or a wizard who's forgotten most of his sorcery, or an ancient, immortal thing no one's ever made up a word for—but to Starling Jane, he's just The Bailiff. A link between the yellow house on Benefit Street and other dark houses in other cities, courier for the most precious packages and urgent messages that can be trusted to no one else.

On the last night before her final rite of

Confirmation, the ceremony on the night of the full Hunger Moon, The Bailiff returns from a trip to New Orleans, and after his business with the dead people upstairs and his business with the hounds downstairs, he takes his dinner in the long, candlelit dining room where the changeling children and the ghoul pups are fed.

"You'll do fine," he assures Starling Jane, nibbling the last bit of meat from a finger bone. "Everyone gets the shakes before their third moon. It's natural as mold and molars, and don't let no one tell you any different."

Sorrow stops picking his teeth with a thumb claw, and "You heard about Lockheart?" he asks The Bailiff.

"Everyone's heard about Lockheart," a she-pup named Melancholy says, and rolls her yellow eyes. "Of course he's heard about Lockheart, you slubberdegullion."

Sorrow snorts and bares his eyeteeth at Melancholy. "What the heck's a slubberdegullion?" he demands.

"If you weren't one, you'd know," she replies brusquely, and Sorrow growls and tackles her. A moment later and they're rolling about on the floor between the dinner tables, a blur of fur and insults and dust, and someone starts shouting, "Fight! Fight!" so everyone comes to see.

Jane keeps her seat and picks indifferently at the green-white mound of boiled cabbage on her plate. "You have heard about Lockheart?" she asks The Bailiff.

"As it so happens, and with all due respect paid to the sesquipedalian Miss Melancholy down there," and he glances at the commotion on the dining-room floor, "no, my dear, I haven't."

"Oh," Starling says and jabs her cabbage with the bent tines of her fork. "He failed his second."

"Ah, I see. Well, now, I'd have to say that's certainly a bloody shame, of one sort or another."

"He was scared. He froze up right at the start, didn't even make it past the sword bridge. They had to bring him down in a burlap sack."

The Bailiff belches and excuses himself. "Was he a friend of yours?" he asks her.

"No," Jane says. "I always thought he was a disgusting little toad."

"But now you're thinking him failing has something to do with you, is that it?"

"Maybe," Jane replies. "Or maybe I was scared to start with and that only made it worse."

On the floor, Melancholy pokes Sorrow in his left eye, and he yelps and punches her in the belly.

"Don't seem fair, sometimes, does it?" The Bailiff asks, and takes a bite of her cabbage.

"What doesn't seem fair?"

"All these trials for them that never asked to be taken away from their rightful mommas and brought down here to the dark, all these tribulations, while others, not naming names, mind you," but Starling Jane knows from the way he raised his voice when he said "others" that he means Sorrow and Melancholy and all the ghul pups in general. "All they have to do is be born, then watch their p's and q's, keep their snouts clean, and not a deadly deed in sight."

"Madam Terpsichore says nothing's fair, and it's only asking for misery, expecting things to turn out that way."

"Does she now?"

"All the time."

"Well, you listen to your teachers, child, but, on the other hand, Madam Terpsichore never had to face what's waiting down in that pit during the full Hunger Moon, now did she?"

"No," Jane says, pushing her plate over to The Bailiff's side of the table. "Of course not."

"See, that's what really draws the line between you and her, Miss Starling Jane. Not a lot of words written in some old book by gods no one even remembers but the hounds, not the color of your eyes or how sharp your teeth might be. What matters—" and he pauses to finish her cabbage and start on her slice of rhubarb-and-liver pie. Jane pushes Sorrow's plate across the table to The Bailiff as well.

"Thank you," he says with his mouth full. "I do hate to see good food go to waste. Now, as I was saying, what matters, Miss Jane, what you need to understand come tomorrow night—" and then he stops again to swallow.

"You really shouldn't talk with your mouth full," Jane says. "You'll choke."

The Bailiff takes a drink from his cup and nods his bald head. Now there are a few beads of red wine clinging to his whiskers. "My manners ain't what they used to be," he says.

"You were saying, what I need to under-stand . . ."

The Bailiff stops eating, puts his fork down, and looks at her, his moss-green eyes like polished gems from the bottom of a deep stream. "You're a brave girl," he says, and smiles, "and one day soon you'll be a fine, brave woman. That's the difference, and that's what you need to understand. Madam Terpsichore won't ever have to prove herself the way you already have. What makes us brave isn't lacking the good sense to be afraid; it's looking back at what we've lived through and seeing if we faced it well. The ghouls are your masters, and don't you ever forget that, but they'll never have your courage, because no one's ever gonna make them walk the plank, so to speak."

And then he reaches into a pocket of his baggy

coat and pulls out a small gold coin with a square hole punched in the center. The metal glimmers faintly in the candlelight as he holds it up for Jane to see.

"I want you to have this," he says. "But not to keep, mind you. No, when you offer your hands up to old Nidhogg's mouth tomorrow night, I want you to leave this on his tongue. I can't say why, but it's important. Now, do you think you can do that for me?"

Starling nods her head and takes the coin from his hand. "It's very pretty," she says.

"Don't you get scared and forget, now. I want you to put that right there on that old serpent's tongue."

"I won't forget. I promise. Put it on his tongue."

The Bailiff smiles again and goes back to eating, and Jane holds the coin tight and watches Sorrow and Melancholy tumbling about on the floor, nipping at each other's ears, until Madam Melpomene comes to break up the fight.

In the dream, she watches the children on the beach with their dog, and the crimson thunderheads piling up higher and higher above the darkening sea. Her mother has stopped talking, and though this has

never been part of the dream before, Starling Jane
turns to see why. But there's no one standing behind
her now, only the tall grass and the wind whispering
furtively through it and the world running on that
way forever.

And then there are no more nights left between
Starling Jane and the full Hunger Moon, no more
anxious days or hours or minutes, because all moons
are inevitable and no amount of fear or desire can
forestall their coming. This is the year of her Third
Confirmation, her time for the Trial of the Serpent,
because she's survived the first two rites, the Trial of
Fire and the Trial of Blades. There are no lessons or
chores on the day of a trial, for Jane or any other
changeling child, and by the appointed hour the
warrens have emptied into the amphitheater carved
from solid stone one hundred and fifty feet beneath
Federal Hill.

    Jane wears the long silver robes of passage and
waits alone with blind, decrepit Master Solace in a
tiny, curtained alcove on the northern rim of the pit.
The air stinks of wet stone and rot and the myrrh
smoldering in a small brass pot on the floor. Her face
is a mask of soot and drying blood, the red and black
runes drawn on her skin by Madam Hippodamia,
that she might make the descent with all the most

generous blessings of the dark gods. From the alcove she can hear the murmuring crowd and knows that Sorrow's out there somewhere, crouched nervously on one of the stone benches, and she wishes she were sitting beside him and it were someone else's turn to stand before the dragon.

"It's almost time, child," Master Solace barks, and blinks at her, his pale, cataract-shrouded eyes the color of butter. "If you are ready, there's nothing to fear."

If I'm ready, she thinks and shuts her eyes tight.

And then the horn, and the ship's bell, and the steady thump-thump-thump of the drums begins.

"Walk true," Master Solace says, and blinks again.

Jane opens her eyes, and the tattered curtain has been pulled back so she can see the torchlight and shadows filling the amphitheater and the pit.

"Walk this path with no doubt in your heart," Master Solace says, and then he ushers Starling Jane out of the alcove to stand on a narrow wooden platform jutting out over the abyss. Above and all around her, the murmuring rises to an excited, expectant crescendo and ghul drum-wraiths hammer at their skins so loudly she wonders that the cavern doesn't collapse from the noise and bury them all alive. That would be easier, she thinks. That would be easier than dying alone.

The drumming stops as abruptly as it began, and gradually the murmuring follows suit, and for a moment or two there's no sound from the great chamber but Jane's heartbeat and Master Solace sucking the dull stubs of his teeth. And then one note rings out from the ship's bell, and "All stand," Madam Terpsichore says, shouting to the assembled through her bullhorn.

"Tonight we have come down to this sacred place of truth and choice to witness the deserved confirmation or the just rejection of Mistress Starling Jane of the Providence warrens. It has been eight years since she was delivered to us by the grace of The Cuckoo, and on this night of the full Hunger Moon we shall all know, once and for all, whether she will serve us until the end of her days."

"Watch your step, girl," Master Solace whispers. "It's a long way down," and then Jane hears the curtain drawn shut again, and she knows that he's left her alone on the wooden platform.

"Go down, Starling Jane," Madam Terpsichore growls. "Go down into the dark and find the hungry jaws of Nidhogg, the dragon that gnaws the very roots of the world tree, drawing ever closer the final days. Find him, changeling, and ask him if you are worthy."

And then the ghoul bows once before she pulls the mahogany lever on her right, and far overhead,

secret machineries begin to grind, the hesitant turning of iron wheels, the interlocking teeth of ancient,
rusted gears, and somewhere on the surface a trap-
door opens, and moonlight pours into this hollow
place inside the earth.

"Walk true, Starling Jane," Madam Terpsichore
says, and passes the bullhorn to an underling before
she sits down again.

The moonlight forms a single, brilliant shaft
reaching from the vaulted ceiling of the amphitheater
to the very bottom of the black pit, argent lunar rays
held together by some clever trick of photomancy
Jane knows she'll probably never learn, even if the
dragon doesn't take her hands. The crowd makes no
sound whatsoever as she turns right and begins her
descent along the steep and rickety catwalk set into
the walls of the pit. And the drum-wraiths begin
drumming again, marking her every footstep with
their mallets of bone and ivory.

Starling Jane keeps to the right side of the catwalk, because she's afraid of falling, because she's
afraid she might look over the edge and lose her
balance. She places one foot after the next, and the
next, and the next after that, walking as slowly as
she dares, spiraling around the pit, and each circuit
is smaller than the last so that the distance to the
moonbeam shrinks until she could reach out and
brush it with her fingertips. The old planks creak and

pop beneath her bare feet, and she tries not to imagine how many decades, how many centuries, it's been since they were anchored to the rock face.

And then, at last, she's standing at the bottom, only one final moment remaining to carry her from the darkness into the blazing white shaft; Jane hesitates a second, half a second, takes a deep breath and lets it out again, and then she steps into the light of the full Hunger Moon.

It's stolen my eyes, she thinks. *It's stolen away my eyes and left me as blind as Master Solace.* This pure and perfect light distilled and concentrated, focused on the dingy, reflecting mirror of her soul. It spills over her, dripping from the silver robe, burning away anything less immaculate than itself. She realizes that she's crying, crying at the simple beauty of it. When she wipes her cheeks, the light dances in furious motes across the back of her hand, and she sees that she hasn't gone blind after all. So she kneels on the stone, and the dragon rumbles beneath her like an empty belly waiting to be filled.

Above her, the drum-wraiths fall silent.

"It's okay," she whispers. "It's all okay," and death's not such a terrible thing now that she's seen that light, felt it burrowing its way into her, washing her clean. On the ground in front of her there are two holes, each no more than a few inches across and ringed with hammered gold and platinum.

And she remembers The Bailiff's coin, gold for gold, and reaches into the deep pocket in the robe where she tucked it safely away before Madam Hippodamia led her down to wait in the tiny, myrrh-scented alcove with Master Solace. Gold for gold, and the hole at the center of the coin is not so very different from the twin mouths of the dragon.

"Just get it over with," she says, and leans forward, plunging both arms into the holes, The Bailiff's coin clutched tight in her right hand.

Inside, the holes are warm and the stone has become flesh, flesh and slime and dagger teeth that eagerly caress her fingers and prick her wrists. Nidhogg's poisonous breath rises from the holes— sulfur and brimstone, ash and acid steam—and Jane opens her hand and presses the coin against the thorny tongue of the dragon. The earth rumbles violently again and Starling Jane waits for the jaws to snap shut.

But then the pit sighs, makes a sound like the world rolling over in its sleep, and there's only cold, hard stone encircling her arms. She gasps, pulls her hands quickly from the holes and stares at them in disbelief, all ten fingers right there in front of her, and only a few scratches, a few drops of dark blood, to prove that there was ever any danger at all.

High above, the amphitheater erupts in a thunderous clamor, a joyful, relieved pandemonium of barks and shouts and clapping hands, howls and laughter and someone ringing the ship's bell again and again.

Jane sits back on her heels and stares up into the moonlight, letting it pour down into her, drinking its impossible radiance through her strangling, pinpoint pupils and every pore of her body, letting it fill her against all the endless nights to come, all the uncountable darknesses that lie ahead. And when she cannot hold another drop, Starling Jane stands up again, bows once, and only once, to Nidhogg Rootnibbler, exactly the way that Madam Terpsichore said she should, and then the changeling starts the long walk back up the catwalk to the alcove. With the applause raining down around her and the moonlight in her eyes, it doesn't seem to take any time at all.

HAVE NO FEAR, CRUMPOT IS HERE!

Barry Yourgrau

ᛦ

Low a boy named Walter came to be all alone in a strange dark house out by a lake on a dark and stormy night, under a full moon, screaming in terror at a very creepy pale little kid also named Walter . . . perhaps this requires some explaining.

Blame it on Crumpot. At least in part.

Crumpot was the name of the unheroic hero imagined and created entirely by Walter. Crumpot starred in vague, goofy adventures that Walter vaguely dreamed up and made vague notes about (mainly the titles, really), in bad handwriting with bad attempts at illustrations, in a notebook that had the decal of a candy bar affixed to the cover with some actual candy bar smudged into it, as a kind of dumbo-clever little semi-joke.

"Dumbo-clever": that was Crumpot and that was Walter. Except Crumpot was in his imaginary twenties (probably?) and Walter was still fifteen. And Crumpot was *massively* dumbo and only *thought* he was clever. He was always wandering across trouble and screwing everything up worse by trying to make it better, and then wandering on to his next date with destiny. Crumpot was too dopey and full of himself to realize just how lame he was. He had a ridiculous little saying: "Have no fear, Crumpot is here!"

Walter cracked up every time he wrote or thought the line. He'd squeeze his eyes shut, his head slowly bobbing up and down: "Have no fear, Crumpot is here!"

Crumpot was a major interest of Walter's right then. Also, listening to his favorite band, Slashpuppy, on his headphones, very loud. *Very* loud. School was low on the interest scale, and it showed.

You'd think all this was so typical for someone of Walter's age and place in life, trudging the endless trudge trudge trudge of eighth grade, that no one could complain.

But Walter's parents did. Walter's father was big on *responsibility*. And the level of *responsibility* aggravation in Walter's life had just taken a serious jump, thanks to Walter's borrowing (without asking) one of his dad's fancy new wrenches to fix his bike. And then dropping or flipping the wrench by the bushes

when he rode off. Really just because he wasn't paying attention—Crumpot's new saga had burst into
his mind: *Crumpot and the Mutant Sprocket Vipers!*

"How *irresponsible* can you get?" demanded Walter's
demanding father.

So summer started and Walter's parents went
away for a week as planned to a business conference;
but Walter was not allowed to stay, as previously
negotiated, at Bobby Sikama's house, which was to
be a trial run for a longer stretch that summer when
Walter's parents went to Italy.

Instead Walter was shipped off to stay with old
friends of his parents out in the country, the Wilkies.
Walter would help Bob Wilkie with a bird census (!);
he would remove his earphones at meals and turn
down the "insane" volume in general; he would finish
a book and be prepared to talk about it (!), instead of
doodling in his "candy-reeking" notebook. Etc., etc.

Either that or be dragged to Italy with his parents and trudge trudge trudge through museums next
month.

"What is it called?" asked his father, in his evil
way. "It's called *demonstrating responsibility.*"

The Wilkies would be grading Walter on it,
making their report at the end of the week. Walter
was on *responsibility* probation.

◆ ◆ ◆

"Have no fear, Crumpot is here," murmured Walter,
silently, unlaughing, *forlorn*, as he rode along in the
old dumpy auto in which Bob Wilkie had picked him
up at the train station. Bob Wilkie had a big flat
kindly face that featured wire-framed eyeglasses and
a dopey hat on his head, like what fishermen wear
in beer commercials. He worked at a company that
made environmentally safe lawn food, or something
bizarre like that. Little strands of hair grew from his
ears. Speaking of ears, Walter had remembered at the
last second to remove his earphones as he got off
the train.

It was a gray, gloomy day. It wasn't warm.
There were lots of pine trees. Bob Wilkie had said,
"Hey, someone's sure grown since last time I saw
him!" Considering they'd met just once, vaguely,
maybe eleven years ago, this was a real piece of
observation. Then he'd said, seeing Walter shiver,
"You gonna be warm enough there, pal? We're
having some strange weather, foggy and nasty.
Who stole summer?" He chuckled. Walter shivered
some more. Then Bob Wilkie sniffed, loudly. "Hey,
what's that smell, like . . . rotten . . . chocolate . . . ?
Candy bar . . . ?" And he peered around at the back
seat, where Walter's backpack lay. Containing Walter's odorous Crumpot notebook.

They drove along past the dark pine trees,
through which showed a gloomy, chill-looking lake.

Shuttered houses appeared every once in a great while, stuck deep in the trees behind crumbly stone walls and entrances. At last they turned in at a particularly crumbly set of pillars, bumped along a driveway through dark towering trees, and pulled up to an old-fashioned house that sat buried under tree shadows. "Home sweet home!" said Bob Wilkie.

Walter blinked at it. This was where Crumpot had brought him: *Crumpot and the Shadowy Tomb of Responsibility.*

As he got out of the car, something shot right past Walter's head so he gasped and jumped. Bob Wilkie chuckled again; then scowled. "Darn bats," he said, squinting up at the air. "Don't know why we got 'em all of a sudden. And what're they doing out in the middle of the day, that's what I'd like to know!"

Walter wanted to know, too. Nobody'd told him about bats: disgusting bats!

Inside the house waited kindly Betty Wilkie, whose face wasn't big and flat, more pointed: birdlike. She seemed to hop around with the nervous energy of a bird. "Look who's grown so big!" she announced, clapping her hands. "Yeah? Who?" Walter wanted to ask.

There was something else, much worse, that nobody had told him about.

"And this is our Walter!" grinned Betty Wilkie. "Sweetheart, come meet another Walter," she said, sickly sweet, coaxing a boy who was half hiding behind her skirt. The kid wriggled out for a moment to stare at Walter. He was about four or so, and puny, with the palest skin and darkest eyes Walter had ever seen. His eyes burned out at Walter from black, shadow-rimmed depths. Walter gulped. He strained to smile, a *responsible* "smile-at-the-little-kid" smile. Betty Wilkie laughed and played with little Walter's long dark-blond curls. "Two Walters; how're we going to differentiate when we want to call one of you?"

"They ever call you Wally?" suggested Bob Wilkie to Walter.

"Wally?" blurted Walter in disgust.

Little Walter stared, and scratched quickly at an inflamed patch on his pale neck. Then he began to whine.

"Poor, poor dear," clucked Betty Wilkie, stroking his curls. "Is neckie hurtems? He's not feeling well these days," she informed Walter. "The precious sweetheart . . ."

"Awful pale, anemic, doctor can't figure it out," added Bob Wilkie. "Poor little fella, he needs to rest."

"I'm not *little,*" snarled the kid, and he scowled, with amazingly savage ferocity, his puny brow all knotted. He actually wailed. "There, there," clucked his parents. "Oh, there, there." Walter blinked in disgust at the little jacket the creator of this obnoxious spectacle was wearing. It was *velvet,* for God's sake.

Up in the dim study that was his bedroom, Walter used his time for "freshening up after the train trip" to sit hunched on the side of his cot with his earphones in, the volume up so high his eardrums ached. "Have no fear, Crumpot is here," a turbulent, murky voice droned in his head. It was a hopeless voice, beyond all humor. Drearily desperate.

Instead of a nice warm lunch, Bob Wilkie took him off for a bird-census session. It was the first part of the responsibility test. It wasn't a huge success. They wandered around through a lot of pine trees and underbrush, with Bob Wilkie suddenly halting, pointing dramatically, and whispering, urgently, "Nuthatch, three of 'em." Or "Scarlet warbler, one—no, two!" Walter wrote names and numbers down in a special census notebook. Of course he somehow managed to drop the notebook in some mud. Then he tripped while crossing a stretch of muddy, mushy bog and spilled and ruined his portion of sandwiches for lunch. So Bob Wilkie had to share his portion between them.

"No problem," muttered Bob Wilkie, licking at every last crumb on his fingers.

He'd been in college with Walter's parents. He was "a truly upright man," in the words of Walter's father. His stomach growled loudly the rest of the session. Walter shivered in his damp sneakers, his mind wandering away irresponsibly to Crumpot country:

Crumpot and the Freezing Bogmen from Hell; Crumpot and the Revenge of the Stinging Nettles—make that Revenge of the Mud-Maddened—Bob Wilkie interrupted by giving Walter the binoculars to hold. Walter fumbled them, and Bob Wilkie and he banged heads, grabbing at them.

"At least you could have brought the sunshine with you!" Bob Wilkie cried, trying hard to joke, as he rubbed his forehead under the crumpled brim of his fisherman's hat.

Not looking so good, that hoped-for month of video games at Bobby Sikama's. Not looking so good.

Back at the house, Walter lay on his cot with his earphones on, and Crumpoted in his notebook. Then he sighed mournfully and dug out the paperback copy of *A Tale of Two Cities* by Charles Dickens (his "reading assignment") and opened it and thumbed and bent it, to simulate reading. Actual reading, through Slashpuppy's din, was of the cheat notes to *A Tale of Two Cities* by Charles Dickens, which Bobby Sikama had loaned him.

Very shortly, he gave up. He needed a walk. He needed a long break. He needed to get away by his lonesome. The Wilkies waved cheerily from the cozy kitchen as he went out the door.

Trudge trudge trudge to the end of the driveway, and with an eye out for bats, trudge trudge trudge off along the road. See Walter trudging under the cold gray clouds, past the dark shaggy walls of the pines. The lake showed for a moment here and there, off in the distance. He lit an *irresponsible* smoke, looking over his shoulder; but the cigarette made him dizzy. He flipped it. Most of the houses were on the other side of the lake, Bob Wilkie had said. Only a few were along here, and most of them were empty till later in the summer. Summer! Walter felt his cold sneakers squelching as he tramped along in the private roar of his earphones. He was miserable. *Crumpot and the Monsters of Misery!*

"*Have no fear, Crumpot is here!*" he screamed at the top of his lungs, up on tiptoe.

At which point a face popped out from the side of the road ahead. It stared at him. It was a girl's face. Walter slowed almost to a stop. The girl continued to stare. Walter advanced uncertainly, and the girl's mouth moved in silence. Walter stopped. He took off his earphones, cut the volume. The girl eyed him from beside a driveway pillar. She had a fierce stare, under dark bushy eyebrows. She was a little older than Walter, and violently pretty. Walter's stomach went funny.

"Sorry?" he mumbled. "I . . . ?"

The girl suddenly pointed down the road from where he'd come.

"I zaid, do you lif zere?" the girl demanded in a thick accent.

"You mean, at the Wilkies'?" stammered Walter,

squinting to understand. "I'm just, you know, staying there. For, you know, a week."

The girl responded to this by scowling suspiciously, running her eyes over him up and down, as if gauging how truthful he was being.

A voice called from somewhere behind her. She swung her head around. She had strikingly black hair. She shouted in a foreign language, gave Walter one last piercing look, then disappeared out of sight.

Walter stood blinking. He shuffled carefully a few feet, and peered down past the pillar, along a driveway. The girl strode toward a man. The man was old and frail-looking, with a gray beard. He wore a tweed suit and a hokey cloth cap. He had a walking stick. He pointed toward Walter watching, and the girl turned around as she reached him, and they both stared at Walter. After a moment, Walter half waved. They didn't wave back. They stared. It was Walter's day to be stared at. After another moment, he edged away from the driveway, and turned back toward the Wilkies' house; but not quite so miserable as before.

Crumpot and the Strange Harsh Beauty . . . When he declared Crumpot's line, this time he didn't shout it, his voice had a funny sort of quaver. But who was she? *And the princess's eyes signaled to him, "Save me from this ancient evil wizard with his black-magic wand thing . . ."*

Was that the trouble she would be in, for Crumpot to tackle?

Dinner that night was spaghetti with some sloppy-gloppy Italian sauce. Good for Walter to get used to, no doubt. The kid hated it. He took one scowling shadow-eyed bite, and then he threw his spoon down and shrank back in the chair and kicked his heels and wailed his pale, puny head off. "Poor sweetheart, you not likems?" clucked Betty Wilkie, hopping over to him to start soothing. "It's got a lot of garlic, honey pie, you used to lovems!"

This made the runt wail even louder.

"Mysterious weak condition makes him grumpy, poor soldier," murmured Bob Wilkie.

When little Walter finally calmed down, his bottomless burning eyes fixed on Walter, who was pointedly continuing to shovel spaghetti down. Sniffling, the kid whispered something in Betty Wilkie's ear. She looked up at Walter and laughed. Awkwardly.

"Walter doesn't like having to share his name with you," she announced.

"Okay, from now on you're *Wally*, that's it," Bob Wilkie informed Walter grimly.

Thought Walter: *Crumpot and the Obnoxious "Wally" of Slander and Doom.*

During the night, things whacked into Walter's window and flittered back and forth outside his curtains under the moon. *Bats?* He shivered under his blanket, trying to focus on the strange fierce girl from his walk. What was that language she spoke? Italian maybe? Maybe? Suddenly museum-month in Italy took on a slight glow. A dog howled, not far away. An endless, bloodcurdling doglike howl, so Walter trembled and wrenched the blanket tighter. A window shutter thumped all at once down the hall, and Walter jerked up and then flung himself as deep into the cot as he could go, burrowing under the pillow, his heart pounding. "Have no f-fear, C-Crumpot is here!" he whispered.

In the morning, he had shadows under his eyes himself. He almost forgot to make his cot, which was part of his *responsibility* program. And a bigger heart-pounder awaited after Betty Wilkie hung up the phone. "That was Barb McIntosh," she announced to Bob Wilkie. "She can't come!" The two of them stared at each other, stricken. Barb McIntosh was supposed to baby-sit little Walter that afternoon and night, when the Wilkies had to go off to a twentieth reunion and special awards ceremony for Betty Wilkie's old sorority.

"But who's going to take care of precious Walter?" she beseeched. (Pale puny Walter was still asleep upstairs.) There was silence, then both she and Bob Wilkie murmured in unison: *"Unless . . ."* And

stepped outside with the pack, so's not to leave tell-
tale odors indoors. A gust of wind blasted his hair as
he squinted about for bats. "Jeepers!" he blurted.

Overhead, the sky was *bizarre*, its low clouds
gray-black but almost yellow, too. They were ragged,
wild, with patches of dark sky (!) showing through.
A pale piece of full moon gleamed a second. What,
it was *evening, already?* The wind stormed again. Walter
blinked through it. Two figures were walking off
down the driveway: a man, a boy. The man's hair
was shiny and dark; his long black cloak swirled in
the wind. The boy had on a little jack—Walter's
stomach dived.

"Hey!" he gasped, hurrying forward. "Hey,
come back!" *Crumpot and the Pedophile Kidnapping?!* Little
Walter and the cloaked man stopped and looked
around. They smiled palely, both of them, toward
Walter. Their eyes flickered red just a moment, like
cats' eyes. Walter gasped and stopped. "H-hey—"
he stammered, a chill climbing his spine. A howl
sounded somewhere to the side. He leaped in fright.

"You *bad* . . ." announced a little voice behind
him. He leaped again, then staggered. The kid was
there—somehow right there now behind him!
Ghastly pale. He smiled up at Walter: the nastiest,
palest little smile Walter had ever seen. His milk teeth
looked sharpened. "I'm Walter," he said.

Walter panted at him, backing away. "G-go

inside, kid——" he stammered. "You're s-sup-posed to be r-resting!" The kid smiled another awful mouthful. "Go in-s-s-side!" insisted Walter. He pointed, trembling. The kid turned, slowly, and *cackled*——and then shot off toward the front door, literally almost flying. The door slammed behind him.

Walter gaped. He blinked. Moaning softly, he peeked a look over his shoulder, down the darkened driveway. The man wasn't there. A big gray dog trotted away into the distance. It stopped a moment and its pale eyes flashed, and it howled. A bat whizzed out of nowhere.

Walter yelped and went careening back to the house. At the front door, he cowered awkwardly, frozen. Inside, what awaited? *Crumpot and the Mini-Ghoul from Hell.* The wind sobbed; it tore at the pines. Walter whimpered and pushed open the door and called into the dark interior: "K-kid?"

No answer.

Walter tiptoed in——and then raced over and turned on the standing lamp. Light bloomed: reassuring, normal almost. The world of *responsibility.* The main room was empty. "Hey k-kid, you resting?" Walter called out toward the stairs, *responsibly,* but involuntarily holding himself shrunk back, like some lame timorous dunce in a horror-movie parody.

"I'm *hungry,*" the little voice announced from above. A spooky little laugh followed.

"I'll make some soup," Walter bleated. "I'll c-call when it's ready. You . . . you rest!"

There was a cackle in reply. Walter snatched up his earphones and cranked them so high, Slashpuppy almost severed his brain. Yes, oh, yes. "Thank you, thank you," breathed Walter's nerves. Crumpot and the Mighty Force of Noise. And now Walter understood: the brat, he could now see, was messing with him. Was trying to spook him, that was it! Was being an agent of the museums of Italy!

Walter gave a trembly laugh, there in the kitchen as he opened a can of soup for the Puny One's supper. "Wally," he sneered. Crumpot and the Treacherous Infantile Creep: The obscene dwarf-menace tried to play with our hero's sanity, but by superior willpower and raw heroic courage . . . etc. Walter got out the Italian sauce for himself, and for a moment considered adding a fat load of it to the brat's soup. But no: he was going to be responsible. He was going to pass Bob Wilkie's big test, and no kid was going to stop him. Crumpot and the—Overboiling Saucepans—

Walter swore and yanked both splattering saucepans off their burners. He sponged away at the mess, pulling his earphones out to concentrate on containing this irresponsibility. The wind surged outside, shutters slammed, a howl went up close by and Walter jumped. The lights flickered. Something was ringing in the main room. The phone! Walter stared at the doorway, remembering that Bob Wilkie said he'd call around dinnertime to check on things! Out into the main room raced Walter. He snatched up the phone. It was Bob Wilkie, demanding was everything okay.

"Everything's f-fine," Walter replied, as the wind wailed outside. Then his voice trailed off, as his gaze lifted toward the stairs. Where a ghastly little figure stood staring at him, eyes red-glowing. "I'm hungry," scowled the brat. Then he smiled, baring a set of honest-to-God fangs.

"What's going on!" demanded Bob Wilkie.

What could Walter say: "It's your precious sweetheart I'm responsible for, he seems to have turned into a fanged ghoul"?

"I'm m-making s-supper," Walter managed to sputter.

"I'm hungry!" insisted little Walter, fangs agleam in the lamplight.

He started gliding down the stairs. The wind howled, Walter slammed down the phone, and all the lights went out. Screaming, Walter raced back into the dark kitchen, banged shut its door, threw the old-fashioned bolt, curled himself at the door's foot.

Something bashed ferociously against the wood on the other side, ferociously scratched and clawed. "I'm hungry!" shrieked the little voice.

"Have no f-fear," whimpered Walter, "have no f-fear, C-Crumpot is here."

"Crumpot, vot ees thees Crumpot?" a low voice demanded in the darkness. Walter yelped. Inside, under the partly open kitchen window, crouched the beautiful girl from the driveway. She crept hurriedly to gaping Walter and the noisy door. "Forget Crumpot, vee must use thees, from my grandfadder!" She showed the walking stick Walter had noticed yesterday. "Sharp vooden stake, through heart!" she hissed. Walter stared, in disbelief.

"Little Walter?" he blurted dopily. A stake through the velvet chest of the precious child, of whose head not a hair must come to harm—his baby-sitting responsibility?

"Hee ees vampire!" snarled the fierce girl.

This talk took place in the midst of continuous assaults on the other side of the door, snarling screeches: "I'm hungry! I'm hungry!" And then, silence.

Walter and the girl stared at each other. "He got tired?" panted Walter. "He went back to bed?" A howl sounded outside. They twisted toward the window.

"No!" shouted the girl.

The window exploded in a shower of glass as the brat burst into the kitchen. Fanged jaws agape he pounced on Walter, who screamed and fell back, flailing, howling himself as sharp things stung his wrist. His earphones were torn off from their resting place around his neck. The girl got behind the little monster and bent back his curly head—back, back. His fangs stuck out pink from Walter's wrist cuts. Over together went the straining girl and little Walter, the kid twisting around and fastening like an insane grunting animal on the girl's neck. She thumped at him, shouting foreign things. They thrashed this way and that. Walter looked wildly for the walking stick, couldn't see it—saw the still-steaming saucepans on the counter. He lurched over to them, came staggering back toward the tussling, spinning bodies. Where to aim? Where to aim? He just heaved, first the molten soup. Screams. Then the Italian sauce. The girl howled. The kid shrieked—he heaved over onto the kitchen floor, flapping like a dying fish.

"*Garlic!*" he squealed weakly, pale and tortured, twitching and twisting. "*Garlic—*"

"Valking stick!" cried the hoarse girl, slumped by the door clutching her bloody, soup-splashed neck. "Vhile hee ees veakened!"

The walking stick. Walter saw it on the floor. He picked it up; he turned with it in a daze. "How do I . . . ?" he began.

"Hurry, hurry," snarled the girl. "Vhile hee ees veak, stab heem in heart—stab heem, stab heem!"

Walter blinked down at miserably snarling, curly-headed little Walter. He raised the walking stick, uncertainly, high over him with both hands. A snapshot flashed in his head: his father brandishing the shiny new neglected wrench high in the air by the bushes, as a symbol of . . . Irresponsibility. Walter, baby-sitting, hesitated. The kid spat at him through his fangs, flapped and flailed with his heels, banged Walter right on his sneakered toe. "Ow!" yelled Walter—and drove the sharpened walking stick down with all his infuriated might. The little demon squealed horrifically, floundering. In agony he clawed as Walter reeled away, hopping. The puny ghastly lips screeched in distress; the puny fingers clawed at the air, clawed at the walking stick buried many inches into the flopping little velvet chest. He began to hiss like a snake. And then he shuddered mightily, and stopped, and just lay there, limp and unmoving in a ghostly ray of moonlight. Pale, like a partially peeled, curly-headed shrimp with a long toothpick stuck in it.

Walter had slain him dead.

Walter slid to the floor, hearing his own stunned gasping. He heard the girl gasping over by the door. "Vot ees dat noize?" he heard her asking eventually.

It was the phone ringing in the main room.

It was Bob Wilkie again, as Walter discovered after knocking the phone over in the dark and fumbling around for the receiver, from which blared, "Hello? Hello! *What is going on, Wally? What the heck is going on?!*"

"Uh, Mr. Wilkie?" Walter gulped, his voice quavering. From on his knees he could see the walking stick through the kitchen doorway, jutting out from the limp baby-sat body. "Mr. Wilkie, uh, I—I don't know if you're gonna believe this about, uh, Walter?" he began.

He had the sinking, sinking feeling IRRESPONSIBLE was going to be his final responsibility report.

Crumpot and the Endless Italian Museums of Soul-Destroying Boredom.

Poor Walter, that didn't half begin to describe it.

⁂

STONE TOWER

Janni Lee Simner

Wind pounded the stone tower, rattling the shutters, finding its way through the cracks between ceiling and walls. Tara shivered beneath thick blankets, listening for—what? She didn't know. She knew only that she was cold, had always been cold.

Wind threw the shutters open, pounded the glass. A bird let out a mournful cry. That call brought tears to her eyes, made her long to answer. She tossed the blankets aside and stood, the carpet rough against her bare feet. Moonlight shone through the curtains. A shadow flew past, dimming the light, letting it through again.

No. The voice was quiet, quiet with rage. *For once in your life, you shall listen.* Tara didn't know where that voice came from; she knew only that she must obey.

To bed. She silently turned and climbed back beneath the covers.

But she could not—would not—sleep. She stared into the dark, listening to the wind, feeling as if she'd lost something important and trying to remember what.

In the morning she went to school.

That seemed wrong somehow, but she did. She descended stone stairs, crossed an ordinary living room with couch, bookshelves, and television, and stepped out to the street. Wind moaned through the bare winter trees, got in around the edges of Tara's thick jacket. The sky was as gray as dying fire.

At school she turned in homework—trigonometry problems, science lab, a paper on Shakespeare. She answered questions, too, whenever she was asked. Her teachers seemed surprised by that, and Tara thought maybe she hadn't always been a good student.

Between classes, people called to her in the halls.

"So sorry—"

"Jeremy—"

"Any news?"

Ignore them, the voice said. *Focus on your studies.* She did as she was told.

At the end of the day someone met her outside the gate. A girl around her age, wearing a crop top and low-riding jeans in spite of the cold. "Hey, Tara. Want to talk?"

"Talk?" Tara searched for the girl's name, couldn't find it.

"You have to talk about this. You can't just—"

Home, the voice said.

"I have to go."

"But, Tara—"

Home!

She ran. The girl followed, calling her name, but Tara just ran faster. Soon she was racing up the driveway to her house, the only stone house in a neighborhood full of cheap wood and peeling paint. She took the tower stairs two at a time, remembering that once living in a tower had made her feel like a fairy-tale princess. When?

She crossed the bedroom threshold, gasping for breath. The door slammed shut behind her. Tara whirled and grabbed the knob, but it was locked.

She wasn't a princess now, only a prisoner. A prisoner with no idea how she'd come to be imprisoned, or why.

Yet the room didn't look like a prison.

The stone walls were covered with ordinary

drywall, painted pink. The carpet was pink, too.
Someone had painted dancing butterflies on one
wall, a trio of rainbow castles on another. An open
door led to a bathroom whose walls and ceiling were
decorated with fluffy clouds.

But even by day the room was cold, too cold.
Tara pushed lacy curtains aside to look outside. Frost
rimed the window; below she saw a winter forest,
gray branches sheathed in ice.

The window was locked, as surely as the door.

Tara pressed her nose to the glass. A raven flew
past; farther off, a wolf howled. Snow began to fall,
landing softly on the sill outside.

Tears flowed down Tara's cheeks. Staring into
that forest made her feel lonely beyond all words.

Someone had left food for her: chicken nuggets,
carrot sticks, frosted cookies. Tara bit into a cookie,
choked on cotton-candy sweetness, set it aside. Outside, the trees were shadows behind a white veil.
Cold as she was, Tara knew the creatures out in the
snow must be colder. The thought brought tears back
to her eyes.

She did her homework, then silently changed for
bed. The pajamas in her drawers were all the same:
thick flannel nightgowns decorated with flowers.

Outside, the wind rose to a howl. As Tara crawled beneath the covers, she wondered if she would ever be warm again.

She dreamed of fire.

Fire brushing her lips, stroking her hair. Fire against bare skin—her skin. She reached for the fire, drew it closer. Skin met skin; warmth spread. Sun streamed through an open window. Tara felt scratchy carpet beneath her, didn't care. Her red hair tangled with another's black hair, sweat-soaked and glistening in the light. Heat brushed her breasts, caressed her back.

Footsteps pounded the stairs; the door flew open with an icy blast of wind. Wind grabbed her, pulled her from the fire. Tara heard a scream, a scream like a bird's cry.

She screamed, too, screamed and woke. Thin morning light filtered through the curtains; cold sweat plastered her nightgown to her skin. Clutching the covers, she walked to the window. The snow had stopped; the world was very still. Outside, something glistened darkly.

A raven's feather, on the sill just beyond the glass.

◆　◆　◆

Tara tried to open the window, but her hands went numb as she struggled with the latch.

Leave it.

The voice pulled her away. Tara got dressed, packed her books and the sack lunch she found beside them. She glanced back at the window.

Go to school.

She went, shivering all the way.

"What's with the clothes, Tara?"

She sat in the cafeteria, eating her lunch—peanut butter and jelly, an apple, a carton of milk. Around her, others ate food they'd paid for at the lunch counter. There was no money in Tara's tower, though, only food and clothing. She looked down at her shapeless sweatpants and sweatshirt. Had she dressed differently once?

"Leave her alone." A second voice, different from the first. Tara looked up and saw a girl in tight jeans and a tighter T-shirt. She remembered a name—Rachel. Rachel and she had been friends since—when?

"You okay?" Rachel whispered.

"Maybe she should see a doctor," someone else suggested.

"Give her time," Rachel snapped. "It's only been two days!"

Bits of apple churned in Tara's stomach. Two days since what? She stumbled to her feet, not sure whether to puke or scream or cry.

Go to class.

Tara fled the cafeteria, ignoring the voices behind her. She went to her afternoon classes, turned in her papers, and answered every question her teachers asked.

When she returned home, she heard a voice singing somewhere beyond the living room. A lullaby, so low she could barely make out the words. She knew them nonetheless:

> *Sleepyhead, close your eyes,*
> *I am right here beside you.*
> *I'll protect you from harm,*
> *You will wake up in my arms.*

Someone had once sung those words to her; she knew they had. A sob escaped Tara's throat, and the singing stopped.

Go to your room. The voice that spoke was the same voice that had been singing. Tara almost recognized it.

Go!

Tara swiftly climbed to her room. The feather

still lay outside her window. She stared at it, fighting more tears, wondering just what she'd lost, and how.

She dreamed of ice.

Ice sleeted against the window outside, frosted the carpet white within. Tara ran a hand through her hair, and icicles fell to the blankets around her.

She dreamed a tall man stood in her doorway, red hair frosted with white, gray eyes cold and bright.

"I love you, Tara." His voice wasn't ice. It was warm, surprisingly so. "Fathers always love their daughters." He entered the room, leaned down as if to tuck her in. Tara trembled, not sure whether she wanted him to draw closer or disappear. He tucked the blankets around her, as if she were very small.

"I seek only to keep you safe." His hand brushed her cheek, sent chills down her spine. Then he jerked back, as if burned. "Your thoughts are with him, even now!" His voice hissed like snow on fire. "I will not lose you. I will not."

He strode away, footsteps heavy against the pink carpet, slamming the door behind him.

She woke to wind. Wind pounding stone, pounding glass. No, not just wind. Something threw itself at her window. Tara leaped up as the thing hit the glass a second time, then a third. A raven, barely visible in the predawn light. Glass shattered, tinkling to the floor. Cold blew through a hole in the window, even as the dark bird spiraled down out of sight. Beyond the hole, glass lay on the windowsill, too.

Glass and a scattering of dark feathers.

There was blood on the glass, and on the feathers, too. Tara walked to school clutching a feather in each hand, knowing the feathers were important, not knowing why. They left red streaks on her palms; when she drew them to her face, they were warm.

Voices greeted her at the school gate. For once she could focus on them, see them.

"Did you hear?" Rachel—her best friend, Rachel—asked.

"The police have widened their search. They don't think he just ran away anymore." Sandra, another friend, not so close.

"My mom says they won't find him alive." Courtney, who wasn't a friend at all.

"Bet even your dad can't hate him now." Tyler, a guy she'd dated once. He'd had cold, clammy hands, and she hadn't stayed with him long.

"I'm sorry," Rachel said. "God, I'm sorry."

A cold lump settled in Tara's stomach. She

didn't want to hear these voices. She didn't care whether she knew them or not. She shoved the feathers into her pockets and ran through the gate.

Her fingers left red streaks on every paper she turned in that day.

She didn't want to go home after school. She wanted to go to the police station. She wanted to ask the police what had happened, who it had happened to.

Home, a voice said.

Her father's voice.

Tara clutched her feathers. For a moment, two moments, she stood stone still.

Then her feet began to move, even as she told them not to. Tara fought, pressing her heels to the ground. She fell to the pavement, scraping her palms, dropping the feathers. Still she inched forward, crawling on hands and knees. Somewhere she heard laughter. Courtney, and maybe Tyler. She bit her lip until she tasted blood, but she couldn't stop moving.

"I hate you," she whispered to the voice.

And I love you. In spite of your willfulness. In spite of your disrespect. Now — home.

Tara stumbled to her feet, grabbed the feathers, tucked them behind her ears. Her sweatpants were torn. She ignored them, placing one foot in front of the other and walking home as slowly as she could.

As she walked she thought of the boy the police had stopped looking for. She suddenly remembered that he had black hair, hair that shone in the summer sun.

At the top of the stairs she stopped short. The bedroom door was ajar.

Downstairs a voice sang,

Lullaby and good night,
You're your father's delight . . .

He'd sung to her. She remembered that now. He'd sung to her, tucking her into a room filled with butterflies and castles. She'd loved him, then.

The bedroom door creaked open. The singing stopped.

To your room. Now!

Tara hesitated, but then she heard footsteps on the stairs. She ran into the room and slammed the door shut herself. She knew without thinking that she didn't want him to see it open.

She didn't want to see him.

Wind blew, making her shiver. The hole in the glass seemed larger than before. Tara looked out and saw a dark shape against the snow below. The raven feathers felt warm behind her ears.

The footsteps grew louder. Tara wanted to hide beneath the pink blankets, hide and never come out. She abruptly remembered that she'd always hidden from her father, once she was older: hidden her friends, hidden clothes and makeup, hidden the things she thought and said and did. Easier to smile and lie whenever he told her to be good.

She leaned toward the window, breathing the outside air, straining for a better look at the fallen bird. Her finger slid along the jagged glass. Tara gasped and drew her finger to her mouth. She'd cut herself, and it hurt.

Wait for me, her father said. *I will care for you. I have always cared for you.*

Tara focused on the pain, found it stronger than her father's voice. She leaned outside, trying to see if the bird was still breathing. She heard her father's hand on the door. *Wait!*

Tara fought that command, drew her fist back and slammed it through the glass instead, again and again, each blow easier than the last. Wind rushed in. Her knuckles bled.

Stop! The door flew open, and her father stormed across the room. Tara couldn't help it—she turned to face him.

He was older than she remembered, lines around his mouth and eyes, more gray than red in his hair. "Tara." His voice was an ordinary voice now, nothing more. "You're my daughter, Tara. I only want to protect you."

She brought her fist to her mouth, swallowing blood, saying nothing.

"It's a cold world outside, child. A cold, dangerous world."

"It's cold in here, too." Tara felt tears against her cheeks.

He ignored her. "I will keep you safe, just like always. There's nothing you need out there."

Tara did look away then, looked to the bird below. As she stared down she knew he was wrong, had been wrong long before—before whatever had happened. "I'm sorry," she said, not sure whether she meant it. Gripping the window with both hands, she swung over the sill, bracing her feet against the stone below. As she did she turned to face him one more time.

He glared at her, all warmth gone. "You will listen!" He began chanting strange, cold words, words she'd heard before, yet words in no language she knew. The blood froze on her hands; ice bound her grip to the sill.

But only her hands were bound. She wrenched them away, one at a time, and heard a sound like shattering glass. Swiftly she descended the tower, ice falling around her, her father's voice fading above.

Memory came flooding back. She remembered

the missing boy's name—Jeremy. She remembered
that she'd been dating him much longer than Tyler,
dating him so long her father found out and told
her she wasn't to see him, wasn't even to speak his
name. Tara didn't listen; she never listened—

She remembered her father, who spent more
time in his locked study than anywhere else. He said
he was a consultant; Tara always knew deep down he
was something more. He was awake all hours, and
sometimes when Tara passed his door she heard him
speaking languages she couldn't understand, couldn't
even find at school to study. He came out often when
she was younger—to sing to her, to play with her.
As she got older she saw him less, and most of the
time he told her only to be good, to behave. Of
course she didn't listen—

Until one day he found her and Jeremy
together, in her room. He began chanting in one of
his languages then. The cold words crawled over
Tara's bare skin, found their way through skin and
blood to bone and thought, to spaces no one's words
belonged but her own. Jeremy screamed and was
gone; a black bird fled through the open window—

Tara screamed, too, but her father's words were
too strong. She couldn't follow the bird. She could
only turn to her father, and hug him, and get dressed
like the good little girl she suddenly was.

The ground drew near; Tara's hands bled once more from gripping the stone. She jumped the last few feet to the ground. The raven had been bleeding, too, but now the blood was dry and clotted. Tara ran to him, saw he was still breathing.

"Jeremy." She stroked cold wings, felt the heart beating beneath them. The bird looked up, and Tara saw recognition in its dull eyes. Sun glinted off its wings, burned against Tara's face. The bird grew warm at her touch, then hot.

She jerked her hands away. Her palms hurt, throbbing pain that ran deeper than the scrapes of glass and stone. She looked longingly at the cool gray walls of the tower. The shutters were closed now, but she knew she could open them. She would always be able to open them.

She took a deep breath and reached for the bird again instead. Heat pulsed through her hands, up her arms, across her chest, and down her back. This time she didn't let go. A burning moment, a flash of searing light—and then the bird was gone. A boy knelt before her, naked and shivering, clutching his broken arm to one side.

"Tara—" His eyes were wild, a bird's eyes.

"Jeremy." She reached out to stroke his cheek, to stroke hair that glistened in the summer sun. His eyes grew bright, fire returning to his gaze.

She drew him close, caressing warm skin, warm lips; feeling his shivering ease. Sun melted the snow around them; wind blew the feathers from her hair. She listened to that wind, listened deep, but in its whispers she heard no voice but her own.

THE PRANK

Gregory Maguire

Y ou might as well come in," goes the old bat at the door, and I go, *You're nuts and I can smell your old-lady b.o. through the screen*, but I keep it to myself, 'cause I got no place else to go tonight.

"You'll be Melanie, then," she says, in a voice like a wasp begging for its life, or a cell phone signal breaking up.

I'll be Melanie till I can be five miles from here, on the freeway with my big thumb out, and then I'll be Titzy Glammer from Alabammer. But to myself. "Yeah, right," like I really could be anyone else, even if I tried. I can hardly even be myself.

"I'm your aunt Beryl," she goes. "Come in." The hand that pushes open the screen has spots big and sucky as throat lozenges. The nose that pokes out at my shoulder height is huge enough to need its own Zip Code.

I slither in. I like to go through doors sideways, opening them as little as I need. It's my way. Don't ask me why.

The room is roasted with old-lady heat, with too many winters of the thermostat pushed up to eighty. The wallpaper hasn't been changed since all the President Bushes were presidential seedlings. Its green vines are faded gray. Golden ovals framing ugly ancestors are stuck here and there. Asparagus ferns wither on rickety tables, praying to die. An old TV with quaint old knobs in the front, like big enough for crippled people to use. Anyway, I see a mouse or something has chewed through the electric wire, so I'm guessing no Fox, no cable, no Shopping Network, no MTV.

"Yeah, like I care," I say to it.

"You'd like something?" Aunt Beryl's eyes are watermelon seeds. Bright and flat and wet. "I'll get you some tea. I'd have come to the bus station if I could, but I don't leave the house."

"I got here, didn't I?"

"That you did." She fusses toward the kitchen, which is like airlifted, time-warped, matrix-reloaded from the early days of television when everyone lived in gray and the mother's hair was a frozen gray perm and her skirts were giant gray starched lampshades and the dads were only gray suits talking superior rightness at their families.

Not even a microwave here. An old gas stove that you have to click something to light.

Aunt Beryl is soft in the elbows. She's padded where she should be bony, and where she should be plump she's sunk or disappeared for good. The look of her would make a light bulb wince. She's nothing like my mom, so I'm going, U R an old bat. Only out loud I'm going, "Is Mom your big sister?" like I must be blind and can't see she's the ancient one.

"Good heavens, no," she says. "Don't you know? I'm your mother's aunt. I'm old enough to be her mother." She takes an old tea bag slouching in a saucer and dampens it with hot water. I'm getting secondhand tea? What a welcome.

She sits me down on a bench built into the wall. The dingy paint on the seat is worn down to wood by decades of shifting, restless behinds. She gives me tea and puts out some things that can't decide if they're cookies or crackers. They're dry as sawdust and taste pukeful. I eat about eight.

"So." She sits down opposite, easing them old bones like they were made of porcelain. "So let's get acquainted, Melanie. Tell me about this thing they call a hate crime."

"Who's gassing you about that?"

"Who's rung up about it? Seems like everyone.

Your mom, for one. The guidance counselor at the school." She smiles as if fondly recalling the one or two phone calls she'd ever received in her lifetime. "That nice fellow from the Department of Social Services."

"Oh, that puff-wocket."

"I beg your pardon?"

I just gnaw on another piece of Styrofoam food product.

"Also the press," she says, more severely. "The press, Melanie. They asked me for a statement."

I raise my right eyebrow, expertly. (I've been practicing to be mysterious for, like, ever.) She doesn't get the prompt, though, so I have to add, "So, like what'd you say?"

"I said I had enjoyed reading newspapers in my day, but had let my subscriptions lapse. I no longer knew how to reply to such a request. I didn't know what was appropriate anymore."

I didn't know if she was being dotty or trying to be funny. But she keeps at me. She raises her own eyebrow like *she* invented mysterious. "A hate crime," she repeats. "I'm not sure I know what that is."

I go, "It was a joke. Nobody can take a joke anymore."

"A joke with a lead pipe and nine stitches?"

"I thought this was supposed to be like a break from all those questions?" I was ripped. "I didn't come here on that smelly-farty bus just to have you jump all over me."

"Oh, I'm not jumping," she goes, "really. I just don't have a television set anymore, not one that works, I mean. And I don't take the papers. So all I know is what Linda Mae—your mom—tells me. And you know how excitable your mom is, especially when she's in custody herself.

"So, really," she finishes, "did you beat up that lesbian girl?"

I go, "I," and then pause, so she gets the idea how rude I think she is, "I don't want to talk about it. In fact I'm supposed not to. This is my vacation."

"This is sanctuary," she goes. "This is to keep you out of a home for troubled teens till your mother is released on bail. This is custody of a minor for a weekend. This is no vacation."

Like, I'm starting to get it, I want to go. I'm *starting to get that*, okay?

"I can, just, go," I go. "I don't have to take shit from you."

"No, you don't," she says, nice as pie. "And I don't have to hold you against your will, either. The state will pick you up if you run away. I won't lock you in here. If you leave, just close the screen against the flies, will you? They're murderous this time of year."

I think the basic idea is she's supposed to be

nicer to me. It's supposed to make me see how real human beings, unlike my mom, behave. I'm supposed to reform by exposure to the good example of good goodness. Aunt Beryl sure looks the part. "You haven't even unpacked yet," she goes, sort of suggestively. "You could be out that door in a jiffy."

"Like you really want me to go."

"I do," she says. She smiles. "Really."

"This reverse psychology crap is so lame. You're so bad at it."

"Honest is honest," she goes. She opens a little drawer in the side of the table. It's got dividers, and there's a slot for knives, one for forks, one for spoons, and a fourth one where she's got a stack of bills in a plastic sandwich bag. She slaps the thing on the table at me. "This would get you started, anyway."

"Give it up," I go. She's starting to creep me out, reality show–time.

"So, you're not going. Not yet. It's there when you want it," she goes. She puts the money back. "Anytime. Now tell me. Where's the hate in the hate crime?"

"I don't hate the bitch," I go, "and it wasn't a crime. It was a prank."

"Oh," she goes. Her voice deepens and softens. "A prank."

"I didn't even know if she's a lesbo."

"That makes it a prank instead of a crime?"

"I mean it was like a party weekend. You know. We were fooling around, me and the guys. There were some beers, like big deal. She was walking home with this Uzbeki transfer student they trucked in from Asia somewhere to make us, like, care or something. Farouza or something. And Farouza was scared of the dark 'cause we stoned the streetlight out, and she's only like been here a month or so, and she told us in class that in her part of Asia they do things in the dark. Bad things, like sabotage and rape and assault and stuff. So really I was like just trying to make her feel *at home*. See? Farouza grabs Delia's hand, and they look like scared lesbos, so me and the boys . . . I mean, it's just for fun."

"Was the lead pipe you picked up particularly funny?"

I don't answer, 'cause clearly she knows the answer and she's just razzing me.

She presses on. "And Farouza? Now?"

"She didn't even get admitted. Stitches and released. She's going to some other school now."

"Nice for her."

"Your sarcasm isn't very, um, sarcastic."

"I don't mean it as sarcasm. Much nicer for her, to go to a school where kids don't attack her. What about this Delia? No permanent eye damage, I hear."

"It's all cosmetic. Like a lesbo can't use a little

cosmetic surgery!" I laugh at my own joke. "She'll have nicer eyebrows the next time she goes into a police station with her parents and *presses charges*."

"Melanie," goes old Aunt Beryl. She sighs like life is too much. "Melanie Pinter. You're too much like your mom. Scary."

"Not much I can do about that."

"You're too much like me," she continues.

"Now *that's* scary," I go. Meaning her to laugh. Maybe we'll start knitting potholders and singing hymns and doing Lifetime-channel bonding stuff.

"It's only for the weekend," she says at last, almost to herself. "The judge is letting your mom out on Monday morning. How like Linda Mae to jump into the fray first and ask questions later. I guess that when the police came to question you, your mom went berserk on them? She must love you, Melanie, though she's more of a fool than you, because she's had a head start and should know better. It's a miracle no one was hurt any worse than they were."

She starts to get up, like the interview is over and I got the job whether I want it or not.

"Just one thing you should know," I said. "There was no hate involved."

"What do you call it if you don't call it hate?" she asked.

I follow her around the house. It's a big old

dump—was probably grand for its time, but its haunches have all fallen and there are cracks in the plaster everywhere. The bathroom tiles are held on by long strips of EXPRESS MAIL tape from the U.S. post office. Everything smells of antique tomcat piss, and there's grit underfoot as if the walls have plastery dandruff. "I sleep here," she goes, pointing at a hopeless flat torture bed on a sun porch, "and you can sleep here." A forgettable room the color of faded celery.

"What's in there?"

"That's off-limits," she goes. "The stairs to the attic."

She tries the door to show me. "See. It's locked."

"Oooh, scary," I go.

"The money's in the kitchen table drawer. Hot water from seven to nine, A.M. and P.M."

"Then what happens to it?"

"I turn off the burner to save on fuel costs."

"No TV?" I go at last. "Really? No working TV? And you never go out? What do you do?"

"I have my chores," she goes. "And there's a nice library lady who comes with her library truck for us shut-ins."

"You don't look like a shut-in," I go.

"Isn't that sweet. You don't look like a hate criminal."

She's peg-legging her way down the stairs, half sideways, to keep her feet flat on the treads. The stairs are old and kind of narrow. "Supper's at five-thirty. Do you like eggs?"

"No, you old creep," I go. "I hate eggs."

"Good," she answers. "We're having eggs."

She reaches the landing and makes the turn gingerly. "The current books are in the parlor. A whodunit and a romance. Also one of those new graphic novels. Very sexy." She sniffs to herself. "I disapprove of the form, but I find I can follow the story better when there are pictures."

So I'm stuck for forty-eight hours, with a maniac prison warden posing as someone's sweet grandma, in a dress that looks like dead, ironed-out pansy blossoms sewn together.

And I read a book, sort of. I eat the eggs. She asks more questions about Farouza and Delia. She's a closet lesbo herself, I'm sure. That's why she never married. Then at nine she turns out the light and leaves me in the dark. "I'm going to bed," she goes.

"And I'm sitting here in the dark?"

"You're not reading anymore, I see, so I'm saving the light bulb."

"Oh." That's the most withering thing I can think of to say; I'm tired.

"By the way," she goes, "the house creaks at night. Old bones, you know. Don't be alarmed."

I don't even bother to answer. I sit there for a while and smell the wallpaper decaying. More little

scrabbles of grit, like there's mice in the walls, but
no sound of mice. (I know what mice sound like.)
Just the hiss and heave of an old house giving off
shavings of plaster as it settles and settles itself into
the dust.

I lie down in the celery room, feeling like a
huge uncooked carrot in there, raw and mean. I'm
deep in sleep and not dreaming about Farouza and
Delia, because why should I, when I wake up with a
start. There's a sound of something, or maybe I mean
there's a sound of nothing. It's like a sound of something with a hand over her mouth.

It is your guilty conscience, girl, I go, because in the
middle of the night words like "guilty conscience"
sneak up on you and bite you where it hurts.

But I hear the sound of nothing to hear, like
stronger than before, and it kind of like freaks me
out, not in a freakazoid sort of way but in a where's-
that-money-in-the-kitchen-drawer kind of way, or a
maybe-I'll-hitch way.

So I get up to use the john. Like there's anyone
to pretend to.

And I let the little light stay on, and I see the
door to the sun porch doesn't fit closed 'cause the
house is not ruled plumb anymore. And unless she's
crouching in the corner like a toddler sucking her
thumb scared of the dark, Aunt Beryl isn't in there.
The blanket is all rucked up, but she's gone.

She's not downstairs. I go check. She's not outside, because the little hook is in the eyelet on the
screen doors, front and back.

So she must be in the attic, right? But the door
is still locked.

And I don't like it much, but what can I do? If
I shriek she'll think I'm freaking out. So I go to bed
and listen to the house clench itself like it has cramps.
And I don't think I can sleep, and I don't mean to,
but I must, because she's knocking on my door and
saying, "If you want a hot shower this morning,
you've got ten minutes before I turn the burner off.
Get up." And it's ten of nine in the morning.

So I shower and we hissy-fit a little at each other
all morning, till she brings up "hate crime" one time
too many, and I go, "Everybody's got a secret, so
that's mine, and leave it alone. What's yours?"

"Oh, tosh," she goes.

"I mean, where were you last night when you
weren't in your room?"

"Tosh," she goes again, but she's a little pale.

"It's already Saturday noontime," I go, "and I'm
leaving tomorrow night, so I'll figure it out."

"You mind your own beeswax," she goes. She
really says that, *beeswax*. I thought that was only in the
old movies. I'm almost charmed.

"Can I go out?" I ask later.

"You know the rules," she goes. "No."

"Everyone's so hyper," I go. "Like I'm gonna find another length of pipe and go nutso in a strange street where I don't even know anyone."

"I know," she goes, "but that's what we agreed to, isn't it?"

"Can I go on the porch?"

She laughs. "I guess I must have some authority, after all. Sure."

So I go on the porch, and what should happen but there's someone from some newspaper lurking behind the lilac hedges, and he asks me what I think about being accused of hate crimes, and am I a victim of backlash or something. I can't follow it, and it feels funny to be interviewed by a lilac bush. But let me tell you that the bush is very very lucky that Aunt Beryl doesn't keep spare lead pipes on her front porch, because I didn't like it when the bush asked me if I would kill again.

"I never killed before," I go.

"Yeah, but your family," hisses the bush.

"Melanie, get in here," goes Aunt Beryl sharply. She's listening from the parlor.

So at dinner I say, "What did that bush mean, my family killed before?"

"It meant nonsense," said Aunt Beryl. "We never killed a soul."

"You're awful interested in hate crimes," I go.

"Eat your eggs," she goes.

"Anything else to eat but eggs in this damn house?" I go.

"There's the money," she goes. "In the silverware drawer. Just clear town, dear, before any more bushes try to interview you."

So I'm tired of the graphic novel—actually, pictures of people with good bodies make me sad and angry. And the romance novel is the same thing only in words; I pick out some passages. The heaving breasts, the powerful arms, the sense of abandon, surrender, deep tremors of feeling no one ever felt before. Right. Makes me feel sad and angry, too. Like, *Who made you so perfect-looking, so deserving of heaving, plunging, throbbing passion?* And also, *Where's my lead pipe?*

And I can't follow the detective story because, frankly, I'm not so good at keeping clues in my head and adding them up. It's a kind of math I can't do.

So I look at some *TV Guides* back from when the TV used to work. They're forty years old and so easy to read, only four channels, no cable. A lot of the shows are the same. *I Dream of Jeannie. Lucy. Bewitched.* Bewitched! Ha.

Then I can't read because, frankly, I'm sort of scared of the house as well as the bushes outside. So I look at cookbooks, *The Boston Baking School* and *Ladies' Auxiliary Recipes*, full of Campbell's canned soup ingredients, with the word *Campbell's* spelled in capital letters every time: CAMPBELL'S. Like the secret name of

God or something. *Take one can of CAMPBELL'S cream of mushroom soup and add one can of CAMPBELL'S cream of chicken soup . . .*

And I find some children's books in the hall, but there were never children in this house, because Aunt Beryl is old and a lesbo and a maiden aunt and a spinster who never goes out. The books must be from when she was a girl. They have cloth spines that smell mildewy, and the pages are thick and creamy like pancakes, and there are liver spots on the pages, just like on the back of Aunt Beryl's hands.

The Secret Garden. Black Beauty. A Little Princess. Girls' books. Yuck, I say, but the pictures are nice. The princess one is all soft and foggy and sad.

I would have read one if I were still a girl, but anyone involved in something called a hate crime (it's nighttime, so I admit it to myself) is definitely not a girl anymore.

But I take it to bed with me, the princess one, because she's all alone I think, in an attic, and she looks sad and like she's never gonna get to be old enough to have heaving bosoms and deep throbbing abandon and muskily go, like, "Oh," and then deeper, "Oh," and then shudder like someone was driving a stake through her heart, only it's not a stake and it's not her heart if you know what I mean, and I think you do.

And I kind of like the picture of the girl in the

children's book better than the graphic-novel girl-
warriors with their rib cages like Batman's molded
plastic and the underwear they flit around in, like
what're they thinking? Like they're asking for someone to come up with a lead pipe and give it to them?

So it's Night Number Two and I go to sleep,
and again I wake up and the house is panicked. The
lights are wavery, as if Aunt Beryl didn't pay the
electric bill and they're trying to decide how much
juice to cut off. The room is hot and sweet and
smells sort of sewery. The screens rule the world outside into microscopic black squares so tiny that the
only thing that can get through is the night. But it
does. And frankly I'm a little fried.

This time Aunt Beryl is asleep. I know because I
look. I see her teeth on the seat of the metal folding
chair she uses as a nightstand. I see a wind-up alarm
clock from before they had batteries. I see a key on a
piece of red yarn, and I know what key it is. I just
know.

It's not hard to get. Aunt Beryl is crankin' out
the zzz's like a comic book. You can almost see her
eyes like two x's, as if someone hit her over the head
and she's out cold. Yeah, with a lead pipe, but I'm
just thinking about it, that's all.

There's no light switch at the bottom of the attic
steps. At the top of the flight, a funny window is set
kind of at an angle. It has four panes of glass, and the

top part fits neatly up into the pointy corner of an eave. The light is bluer up here, as if all the darkness of night has pooled down by the talking lilac bushes and the scary screens in the windows, and up here, though it's hotter than hell under the roof tiles, the colors are cooler.

There's a top landing, a turnaround point, and two doors. One of the doors is low and looks like it goes to a crawl space for trunks and junk. The other door is part open and there's a, yeah, you know it, a glow. A *glow*. Bluish.

I keep waiting for Aunt Beryl to scream at me from the bottom of the stairs, and go, "NOOOOOOOOOOOOO-OOOOOOOOO!" in a slow-motion basso-profundo sort of way. But she's still in there sawin' *zzz*'s. She sleeps like a trucker.

I get to the door. The floorboards were painted once upon an eternity ago, but they're mostly worn splintery now. The door is up and down planks, nothing fancy. Why am I focusing on the floorboards and the door? 'Cause I don't really want to look inside and see what's there.

But you know what? I'm leaving tomorrow night, Monday morning at the latest. So what the hell. I poke my head around like there's going to be some creature hooked up to a computer, or swarms of beetles on a vampire corpse, or something.

What it is—takes my eyes a moment to

adjust—well, far as I can tell, it's like a young Aunt Beryl. A young woman with the same sort of unfortunate shark-fin nose, but her hair is brown and long, not white, and pulled back around her head with a cloth or a rope or something.

The smell is foul, like I imagine a hospital ward might be, and no minty air-freshener strips dangle in the windows.

The young woman turns, and believe me, you never saw anyone tiptoe and scram so fast at the same time as I manage to do. And the sound I hear is like the sound a chicken would make if it is in the throat of a snake. Or a snake would make if it is choking on a chicken. Or both at the same time.

Believe me, I lock that door. I drop the key where it was. I don't care if Aunt Beryl hears me now. I want her to wake up.

But she's a stubborn old cuss, and she doesn't wake up. So I go back to bed and sit up most of the night, scared to sleep till the night drains back out of the room through the screening. Like the tide going out.

"Ten minutes till shower cutoff time," she's going, cheery as a bat, and I realize I have slept. I shower. I feel like I dreamed the whole thing. But then why the locked door?

"For lunch today, since it's Sunday," she goes, "how about eggs?"

"Aunt Beryl," I go, "who is in that bed upstairs? In the attic?"

And you'd've thought I smashed her across the temple with a lead pipe.

"Who said you could go upstairs?" she goes.

"Nobody said it."

"How'd you get the key?"

"I got it. Who is it?"

She looks sullen, like she's pretending a little-girl face, her lower lip pushed out. I guess she's biting the inside of her mouth.

"You dreamed it," she goes.

"Prove it," I go back at her. "Take me upstairs right now and show me she's not there."

"You have no right," she goes.

"Yeah, tell it to the talking bush," I go.

So that shuts her up, and we eat our eggs as if we like them.

"It's Aunt Letitia," she finally goes.

I go, "First I find out you're not Mom's sister, then I find out Mom has a sister, after all."

"Aunt Letitia is not Linda Mae's sister," she goes.

"She's not your sister," I go. "No way. She's not so—" I try not to say old. "Decrepit," I say instead.

"No," goes Aunt Beryl in a small voice. "No, you're right. She's not my sister."

"Well, what's she doing locked in the attic?"

Aunt Beryl looks up. Her face looks like a small

change purse that got turned inside out and there's nothing left inside, and you can see all the puckers of the lining and the lint and where the fabric is worn to threads. "Aunt Letitia is my aunt," she goes.

"Oh," I go, "excuse me for having nothing better to say to that load of crap but, I mean, puh-*lease.*"

"Police?" she says worriedly.

"Please." I spell it out. "Puhl-leeze."

"Oh."

"But she's not much older than me?"

"Oh, yes, she is," goes Aunt Beryl. "She's quite a bit older than you."

So she tells me the story.

Aunt Letitia is something like eighty years old.

She's a farm girl. You can't say she *was* a farm girl because she still is.

So she was Aunt Beryl's aunt on some family farm I never heard of out toward Skaneateles. And Aunt Beryl was growing up in the big city—Troy, New York—but spending summers on the farm. And one summer when Aunt Beryl was round about my age (naturally, otherwise this story would have no point), she did something real bad. Real, real bad.

Badder than anything with a lead pipe. Believe me.

She doesn't say if she did it alone or with a friend. My guess is with a friend, and she's carrying the secret to her grave. If she ever gets there.

What happens is, there's problems that summer with rats, because of bad rains or something, and instead of hanging out in the barn stealing the grain, they keep coming in the house for some reason. And young Aunt Beryl is scared of them. And Aunt Letitia makes fun of her city niece Beryl, can't put up with a few harmless creatures of Gawd! She makes fun of her maybe once too often.

So Beryl, who has more spunk than she shows, puts just a little rat poison in the sugar bowl. She knows how much is too much, because she's been watching them sprinkle it to keep the rat population down. She knows Letitia's the only one who takes brown sugar on her morning oatmeal. Everyone else takes salt and milk.

"Just enough to make her throw up and feel punky," goes Aunt Beryl, some fifty-odd years later. "The way she made me feel." Still somewhat defensive about it.

But something goes wrong.

"She falls into a coma like Sleeping Beauty and never wakes up?" I go. "Really. Really, Aunt Beryl. You working with D.S.S. on some kind of horror story to scare me straight? It won't work."

"No," goes Aunt Beryl. "A coma actually might have been better. Kinder."

"So she wakes up?"

"After a fashion."

"And—what? She stays youthfully gorgeous the rest of her life? What's so wrong with that?"

"If that was all it was," goes Aunt Beryl.

"Show me. Tell me," I go. "I have a right to know. Does Mom know?"

"Of course not." Aunt Beryl is sort of snappy. "Your great-uncles knew, but that was it. And I've spent my whole life in this house taking care of her. For my crimes!"

"Hate crime," I hiss. 'Cause sometimes you can't pass up a good opportunity.

"You said it," she answers. "They didn't call it that at the time, because the family never admitted what happened. They said she went on a holiday to the city and was drowned in a ferry disaster or something. Of course there were rumors. Of murder. Murder might have been kinder."

"Murder kinder? Kinder than what?"

She's reading the past on some text screen inside her head; she doesn't hear me. "Then the war came, the Second World War, and everyone was conscripted. Those young men who came back whole, or nearly so, never came knocking for a date. So the family dies off and dwindles down to me. And your lot, too, Linda Mae and you. What good you are."

"What good are you?"

Then we begin to fight. I mean, it's a nice day, the money to leave is still in the drawer, there's still something a little true about this story, 'cause there was something weird and unworldly about Aunt Letitia. But Aunt Beryl won't take me up there to see her again and she won't and she won't.

So eventually I just take the iron skillet and say, "I've had it with the eggs," and clobber her a little bit on the noggin. Just a little. Now she really does have x's in her eyes, almost.

"It runs in the family," I tell her form on the grimy red-and-white squares of the cracking linoleum floor. I take the key from around her neck and think, *Well, okay, how scary can an old relative be at three in the afternoon on a Sunday? Gawd's day, for Crissakes.*

I don't creep. I don't tiptoe. I just barge up and tromp around. Angry at the whole world, already angry at myself for clocking Aunt Beryl. There are four panels of blue sky at the head of the stairs, little skeins of cloud marbling through like fat in bacon. The floorboards creak differently in the day. I'm noticing again because I'm slowing down.

But hell. I can leave in a minute, take the money and bail out exactly sixty seconds from now if I want.

So I just go in.

There are shades at the windows, tacked down with that same post office tape. The room is yellowy today, 'cause the shades are old. There is a plate of— you guessed it—eggs, largely uneaten, on a side table. A big plate. A platter, really. No, a fancy pasta bowl, the kind with shallow, sloping sides, big enough to serve a family of six. That's a lotta eggs for one young woman with a shapely head and a nice expression in the eyes.

The eyes are open this time. Her head turns a little. The eyes look like my mom's: very black and inky, depthless, or with steep depths it's hard to read.

Her mouth opens in a kind of a yawn. I guess she was napping.

"Hi, I'm your cousin-thingy, your niece. Melanie Pinter," I go.

The voice sounds like a pterodactyl having its nails pulled out by Dr. Torture using a pair of red-hot tongs. I almost brain myself backing up against the wall. I see now that the rope holding her hair into a knot actually isn't. It's tying her to the bed.

"She's a monster!" I go, though whether I'm talking about Aunt Beryl for tying her own relative to a bed, or whether I'm talking to myself about Aunt Letitia, frankly I couldn't tell you.

How does she have the strength? I go to myself. That little, frail Aunt Beryl is yanking knots around bed-posts? No wonder she sleeps so hard at night! She's working like a stevedore during the day.

I hear Aunt Beryl stirring. She's closer than I realized; she's pulled herself to her feet down there. Maybe she's starting up the lower staircase. "Melanie?" she goes. Beseechingly. Falsely?

"Leave me alone," I go.

To the young woman on the bed with the scared eyes and the industrial-strength sore throat, I go, "I'll get you out. I'll *get you out*."

"Don't go near her!" goes Aunt Beryl.

"Come on," I whisper to Aunt Letitia. I grip the tired old army surplus blanket, which is frayed, so frayed! Ripped into shreds! Aunt Beryl is a monster, not even providing a decent blanket!

I pull it down so I can get at the ropes, loosen them, free her. We can run away together. We can push past Aunt Beryl and take the money and get on a bus and get the hell out of here.

I see why the blankets are torn. The ropes— God, I scream; I sound like Aunt Letitia cawing; it must run in the family, that scream—the ropes are knotted two, three times around Aunt Letitia's wrists. Only they're not wrists, really; I don't know what you'd call them. Sort of twists of cartilage ending in claws. Limbs, I guess, with rank, flea-rich hair, stinky as a wet dog. There's something of a nightgown wrapped around her upper torso, but her lower limbs are naked and secured by ropes to the posts of the footboard. They're the limbs, I guess I'm supposed to think, of a rat. I never actually saw a rat before, except in movies, where they're probably computer animated.

Only, Aunt Letitia isn't computer animated, but

she is as frightened of me as I am of her and is scrabbling to break loose. That cry, that screech, comes again and again. Little clots of plaster break loose from the walls, as if the whole house wants to fall down around her, but can't yet.

So I didn't run away with Aunt Letitia, as you probably guess, and I wasn't put in jail for hate crimes against lesbians, Delia and Farouza, and I didn't kill Aunt Beryl, because she showed up on the top floor at last, and we cried, all of us, Beryl and Letitia and Melanie. We held each other tight as ropes could do, because we had no other choice in the world.

And Mom got out on bail 'cause her boyfriend liked her that week, and she came and got me Monday morning. On time, for once. I never said a word, not a word. Because I know Mom isn't smart enough to deal.

I am totally zonked out. I sleep in her boyfriend's stinking car all the way home. I didn't promise to come see Aunt Beryl again. Frankly, I hope I never do. Who could put up with all those eggs?

I hoped when I woke up and got home, I'd have a new life. I hoped I'd think it was all a dream, a delusion. I didn't know if that would happen. I just slept. And not to know I'm alive is kind of a help.

I was tired, like I said. I had stayed up all night, long after Aunt Beryl went to bed downstairs to her punishment cot on the sun porch. I sat near Aunt Letitia, as close as I could bear. I read her as much of *A Little Princess* as I could. I didn't know if she would like it, or if she understood English anymore. But it was about a little girl in an attic, and someone came to save her. And we can all hope.

WRITING
ON THE
WALL

Celia Rees

Mark Banks had a tendency to act on impulse; otherwise he never would have bought the place. The house stood back from the road, in the hollow of a hill. He glimpsed it through a haze of new green leaves, picked out by a random shaft of sunlight on a bright spring day. He noted the FOR SALE sign and pulled in to take a closer look. It was built from dull red brick, not particularly picturesque, but gable ends and steeply pitched roofs, banks of tall chimneys, and a fancy turret gave it a certain grandeur. A Victorian gentleman's residence. He liked the idea of that. The FOR SALE sign had been up for so long that the post was rotting, but he didn't question why that might be. He merely noted the estate agent's number and decided to give them a call. He had to smile when they told him the price. He put in an offer right over the phone. He knew a bargain when he saw one.

There was something hidden about the house, tucked away in a nook of the landscape, folded in on itself as if guarding a secret, the twin roofs of the gables rising like great arching brows frowning a warning, but Mark was not a man given to fancy. His son, Sam, was far more sensitive. He felt a definite prickle of doubt the first time his dad showed him the photographs, but he didn't share his misgivings with anyone. Who'd listen to a twelve-year-old?

There was a lot of work to be done, Mark told his family, but it was going to be fun. The estate agent had recommended a good local firm, and they were already transforming the place. The fabric was sound, the survey said, and that was enough for Mark. There are other sorts of rottenness: kinds that can't be detected by gauges measuring dampness or gadgets that find dry rot or woodworm infestation, but Mark Banks didn't stop to think about that.

He was due some time off and had decided to oversee the work himself. He liked getting his hands dirty and had definite ideas about how the place should be. There were interesting features, like a pretty little summerhouse in the garden, and there had been some fascinating finds already. Just yesterday, one of the men had found a little glass bottle, half filled with some dark, viscous liquid, hidden above the doorway. None of them seemed to know what it was, or why it was there. Mark planned to take it to the local museum as soon as he could find the time.

He'd fixed up a trailer in the garden, and now that school vacation had started, the kids would be joining him. They were both curious to see the house. Kate was fifteen and had already picked out her room from the photographs. She wanted the turret because it looked like a tower in a fairy-tale castle, and she'd wanted to sleep in one of those ever since she was a child. Not that she'd be moving in for a while. She'd be staying with him in the trailer. It was big enough for all of them, but Sam said he wanted to sleep outside so he could try out his new tent.

Sam liked the idea of camping, but on the first night he found it hard to sleep. He wasn't used to the quiet, and each time he closed his eyes, there would be some unfamiliar noise: the hooting of owls or the sudden, sharp shriek of a fox. There were rustlings, also, and other odd sounds that were hard to identify. He stuck his head out and shone his flashlight around, but the little pool of light only made the surrounding darkness blacker somehow. He was aware of the huge bulk of the house looming above him. It seemed to grow outward, radiating blackness, overshadowing, reaching toward the dim, tinny shine of the trailer. That seemed farther off now, like a toy. Suddenly, it looked very small, as if seen through the wrong end of a telescope. He could knock on the door and demand to be allowed in, but then they would know he was scared. That was not the only reason. He could not leave the tent. He was gripped by a panicky feeling—he might not make it in time. Make it from what? There was nothing out there, he told himself. It was a hot night, but he made sure to zip the flap tightly. He could make it through just one night, he thought, as he huddled down into his sleeping bag.

Things look better in daylight. In the morning, Sam didn't like to admit his fear. He moved his tent, pitching it next to the trailer, rationalizing away his night terror, coming up with things Dad might say: too much imagination brought on by difference, strangeness, a change in environment.

Eddie Mayer drew up in his truck, going through the jobs for that day in his head. He scanned the brooding façade of the house. He knew all about its history. His great-grandfather had been one of the builders involved in the Edwardian renovation. He'd been a bit of a cunning man. Eddie wouldn't mind betting that he'd been responsible for the witch bottle they'd found last week. It would have been put

there to protect the building from evil, and if anywhere needed protecting, this place did. Eddie had
been surprised when Haslet and Jones sold it. The
house had been on the market for ages, and with
good reason, but then this London chap comes
along. Old man Haslet had tipped him the wink,
because there was a lot of work to be done, enough
to keep Mayer & Son busy for months. There were
plenty of stories, all right. He would not like to be
here at night. Not that he'd be saying anything, and
neither would his men. The new owner might take
fright, and Eddie had already bought the materials
and taken on extra workers. He could do without a
canceled contract.

Tom Mayer jumped down from the truck. He
was tall and dark, well muscled and tanned from
working with his father. He knew the work, the
business, but he was going to college, and after that
he planned to get a white-collar job. He had no
intention of doing this for the rest of his life. Not
that he'd told his father. It would break the old
man's heart. What was more to the point, he might
not hand any more money out, and Tom was always
short on funds. Eddie might even take away his car.

"Would you like some tea?"

Tom smiled down at the girl offering him a
mug. Not very old. Fourteen? Fifteen? She'd be pretty
if she wore her hair different and lost the braces.

Nice eyes, though, and those shorts and crop top really showed off her figure. Things were looking up.

"Hi, I'm Tom," he said. His smile grew wider and he crinkled his dark blue eyes.

"I'm Kate. Kate Banks."

"Hi, Kate. You weren't here last week."

"No. I came on the weekend with my brother. We're helping Dad. Spending the summer . . ."

"Bit boring for you." Tom folded his arms and looked sympathetic. He made his mind up quickly about girls and didn't waste time. "Tell you what. There's a barbecue tonight in the village. Want to come along—meet some people?"

"Yes," Kate said. She was so taken aback by his invitation, she'd agreed before she'd even thought about it. "That's if Dad says it's okay."

"He can come. Your brother, too. It's a family thing." Always a winner, that. He looked around. His dad was shaking a shovel and pointing at the house. "That's me. Gotta go. Thanks for the tea. See you later."

Kate walked away, smiling to herself. He was all right! Only been here a day and she'd gotten a date. What would the girls think about that!

Sam adjusted his facemask against the fine plaster dust billowing from the sitting room. The ground

floor was being systematically stripped. The house
was far older than it looked, Eddie said, and Dad was
interested in uncovering some of the original building. If the theory was correct, there should be a
bigger, more ancient fireplace behind the Victorian
grate. All work had stopped as everyone gathered to
see if Eddie was right.

"Okay. Stand back!" Eddie spat on his palms and
hefted the sledgehammer.

The thick muscles bulged in his shoulders and
arms as he dealt the chimney piece such a mighty
crack that the whole house shook. Everyone jumped
back as plaster and rubble poured across the room,
sending up a great plume of dust and soot.

"Come on," Eddie shouted, appearing like a
ghost through the choking cloud. "Get this lot
shifted."

"What the—"

The workman dropped his shovel, backing away
from the thing as it bounced and skittered over the
scree of plaster. The dried-up body of a cat. Tufts of
black fur still mottled the brittle blue-gray skin as it
lay stretched, the bone-thin back legs flexed, front
paws extended, blunt head up, as if it had been set to
hunt through eternity.

"Well, I'll be . . ." Eddie removed his mask and
licked his black-rimmed lips. "Haven't seen one of
them in a while."

"Where did it come from?" Sam asked, staring at the pathetic little corpse.

"From the chimney," Eddie replied.

"How did it get there?"

"Dunno, son," the builder said with a shrug. "These old chimneys are full of nooks and crannies. Probably crawled up when the fire was out, for warmth, and died of fumes when someone lit the coals."

It seemed a good enough explanation, but Sam could tell that he was lying by the way his eyes shifted, by the way he licked his blackberry lips.

One of the men went to shovel up the remains with the rest of the rubbish, but Eddie ordered the thing to be burned. Any protection the creature might have offered was gone now, but that was no reason to treat it with disrespect.

Eddie set to work shoveling the rubble out, while the rest of his men dispersed to work in different parts of the house. Tom had been sent upstairs to see what needed doing up there. Curiosity more than any instruction from his father took him to the little turret room at the end of the second-floor corridor. The house was haunted, so they said. This room was where it was supposed to kick off. He stepped inside and looked around. There was no physical evidence of violence and sudden death. He stood, waiting.

To his intense disappointment, he felt absolutely nothing. Not even the slightest shiver. No sign at all of the psychic activity that was supposed to circulate from this very room.

He went to the window and looked out. Nice view. Kate was sunbathing on a patch of grass below. You could see even more of her figure now. He'd seen the other men looking at her . . .

He pressed the window frame with his thumb. The wood was soft. Rotten underneath the paint. The whole thing would have to be replaced. He blow-torched a patch of paint to find how bad it was, how far it spread. The layers bubbled back, turning from yellowy-white to brown and then black. He scraped away at the goo and put his mask up against the acrid fumes. His father was right to be strict about that—they'd used all kinds of poisons to make paint back then: lead, arsenic, you name it. His eyes strayed back to the girl and stayed on her a long time. He was finding it hard to concentrate. She shouldn't be showing herself off that way where the other men could see. It wasn't right. Her dad should have a word with her. Or he would—he would tell her tonight . . . He stood there, brooding. Jealousy and anger growing within him. He shook his head, trying to clear it. He'd only just met her, and he was thinking about her as though she were his girlfriend or something. Maybe the fumes *were* getting to him. He pulled his mask tighter. It was almost as though his thoughts belonged to someone else.

He stayed only a little while longer, but by then the damage was done. No kind of mask could protect against the poison that seeped from the fabric of that particular room.

Sam had been looking forward to the barbecue, hoping to meet some kids his own age there, but most turned out to be younger, so he stayed with Dad. Sam wished he were old enough to join Kate and hang out with Tom and his friends drinking beer. That looked like more fun—although he'd be annoyed if he were Kate. Tom had seemed like a nice guy, pretty happy-go-lucky, but he obviously had another side to him. He kept her close, as if they'd been going out forever, and he didn't like it if she went away from him or talked to anyone else. She seemed okay with it. When Tom's friends moved to their cars, ready to go somewhere, she came to ask Dad if she could go with them. He said that she could, as long as she wasn't back late.

Sam didn't know how late it was, but he was woken up by a door slamming and what sounded like a sob. A car drove off, engine roar and wheel spin ripping through the silence. The trailer door opened and Dad called out, sounding anxious. Kate replied to him, and Sam heard her go in. Or at least, he thought he did.

When Sam woke again, he was dying to pee. He crawled out of the tent, urgency quelling any fears he might be feeling. He wasn't scared anymore. Moonlight made tonight quite different. It was pleasant to be outside after the stuffiness of the tent. He wandered up toward the top of the garden, looking at the stars.

That's when he saw them.

They were in the ruined summerhouse. Lit by moonlight. Two people standing close enough for their shadows to almost merge. Sam stood transfixed. One was taller, bending down toward the other. He could hear them murmuring, whispering, and then the shadows joined into just one shape. He found it hard to tear himself away. It must be Tom and Kate. Maybe they'd had a fight or something, and were getting back together. But he'd heard her go into the trailer, he was sure. How had she sneaked out again without disturbing Dad?

Not that Sam had much of a chance to find out. The next day, Kate stayed in the trailer. When Sam asked what was the matter, she refused to answer. Dad said he didn't know either, but he looked as though he wished Mom were here.

There was no sign of Tom.

"Stayed at his friend's house and hasn't turned up this morning," Eddie said. "If he weren't the son and heir, I'd fire him." The builder laughed and ruffled Sam's hair. "You'll have to do instead."

Sam spent the morning with Eddie, but by the afternoon he had tired of the dust and noise. He mounted the stairs to get away from it. The upper floors would be deserted and quiet. He hadn't really explored up there.

Sam looked along the dark-paneled corridors leading off from the first landing and decided to take the left-hand passage, pushing doors open one by one. Most of the rooms were empty, with bare wooden floorboards and chipped skirting boards. The old furnishings showed as darker patches on the wallpaper, like ghostly imprints of the former inhabitants.

The room at the end was round, like a turret. Light shone through the open door, spilling bright into the tunnel-like passage. Sam squinted, trying to see better. There seemed to be someone in there. A girl standing at the window, facing out, away from him. She raised her arms, the light around her breaking into shafts in the dust-laden air. It was hard to see because of this halo effect, but it had to be Kate. What was she doing up here? It was the room she wanted, so perhaps she'd come to inspect it. But how did she get past him? He looked around, as if to check his route again. When he turned back, the room was empty. The girl was gone.

Sam went in cautiously, searching the room carefully, looking for a secret passage or stairway, but if there was one there, he failed to find it. He was about to go, when he noticed something. Something on the wall. He hadn't noticed it before. It was as if it had suddenly appeared. Strange. Weird. He'd have to tell Kate.

He found her in the trailer, reading a book.

"How did you do it?" he asked.

"How did I do what?" she replied without looking up.

"Get out of the room without me seeing."

"What room? I don't know what you're talking about."

"Yes, you do. The little turret room. I saw you up there."

Kate looked up. "I've been here all afternoon reading this book."

"Well, okay." Sam didn't believe her, but stopped short of calling her a liar. "But you better come. There's something you ought to see."

"Aren't you a bit old for writing on walls?"

"It wasn't me! I swear it! It just appeared . . ."

The writing was a jagged scrawl, the letters at least a foot tall.

KATE

PLEASE

"And I'm supposed to think you've got nothing to do with this?" Kate turned on her brother. "Yeah. Right!"

"Tom was up here yesterday." Sam spoke cautiously, sensing Kate didn't want to talk about him. "Maybe he—"

"No. Why would he?" Her tone was cold, dismissive.

The writing was malformed. There was something hideous about the straggling, spidery letters. Why would Tom do that? It was easier to believe that Sam had done it, even though he was telling the truth and Kate knew it. She grabbed a loose corner. The sheet came away, buckling to the floor. There was more underneath.

I AM TRYING

Kate worked away at the edges of the paper with her fingernails, pulling it off the wall in strips.

On the layer below was more writing in the same spiked hand.

LISTEN

TO ME

"The men are leaving," Sam said as he looked out of the window at the sound of the truck. "It's getting late. Dad's waving us down to go into town."

"You go. I want to get to the bottom of this."

Kate went to find some kind of scraper and came back with a chisel and a trowel. The writing both intrigued and disturbed her. She'd thought at first that maybe it was Tom, but now words were appearing below the surface layer. She worked in the still quietness of the deserted house with single-minded intensity, seeing only the patch of paper before her. She put the curls of paper on the floor as she found them. Maybe a girl named Kate had lived here once. It was a common enough name, after all. These messages must have been left for her by some other person. That had to be the explanation. Someone who didn't write very well. A servant, maybe. Lots of people couldn't write back then. Or someone who had to use his or her other hand for some reason, perhaps because of a broken arm or something . . .

◆ ◆ ◆

Sam had not wanted to leave Kate in the house on her own, but he knew it was no use arguing.

"Where's Kate?" his dad asked.

"She doesn't want to come."

Mark Banks shrugged, not surprised. Kate had been in a mood all day.

"I don't think we should leave her—" Sam started to say, but his dad interrupted him.

"Why not? She's a big girl now, and I don't have time to argue. I've got things to do. I want to catch the museum before it closes. They've got some news for me."

"About what?"

"That bottle the builders found."

Sam settled back in his seat. That sounded interesting. Some of his concern for Kate slipped from his mind as his father headed into town.

The young curator was there to meet them. She'd prepared a written report on their find. Sam craned to read it over his father's arm.

> **Witch bottles** may be of glass or pottery and are usually found concealed beneath the hearth or threshold, but sometimes in walls or beneath the floor. Upon analysis, these bottles have most commonly been found to contain iron, in the form of pins or nails

(often bent), human hair, and urine. All of these sub-
stances have associations with folk magic and together
would seem to constitute a kind of spell. The locations
in which these bottles were placed are significant.
There is an emphasis on placing the objects at the
entry and exit points of the building to serve as protection against supernatural forces that might want to
invade the premises.

The curator held up their bottle, agitating it
slightly.

"Your find pretty much conforms to the norm
as far as contents are concerned. Have there been any
more finds of a similar nature?"

"They found a dead cat yesterday," Sam said.

"Did they?" The young woman turned her vivid
blue eyes on him. "Where exactly?"

"In the chimney."

"Now that's interesting. The finding of dried-
up cats in buildings is quite common," she said,
addressing both of them. "Some may have died naturally, but there is ample evidence to suggest that
many of these poor creatures were deliberately placed
at significant points, particularly the chimney or
hearth, and that they were put there as some form
of protective magic. Cats were widely believed to be
gifted with sixth sense and to have psychic awareness. So maybe they were put there so that they

could exercise their psychic ability and hunting prowess as spiritual protectors of the house. That's what I think, anyway. Were the remains kept, by any chance?"

"No." Mark Banks shook his head. "Disposed of, I'm afraid."

"Pity." The young woman frowned. "That's the difficulty. People don't hang on to them. Too yucky. They usually end up in the trash." She looked up at Mark. "I don't suppose you'd be willing to donate the bottle to the museum?"

Mark smiled. "I'd be delighted!"

"Oh, good." Her face cleared, and she smiled back at him. "Where is the house, by the way?"

"Just out of Stoneham. On Amershed Road. It's set back a bit—"

"The Pearson house?"

"Why, yes."

"Oh, that explains a lot. The house has something of a history. There's a famous ghost story attached to it. Didn't you know?"

Mark shook his head.

"What happened? In the story, I mean," Sam asked, gripped by a creeping dread.

"Well, you know the turret room?"

Sam nodded, his unease growing.

"A young girl died there in Victorian times. She was found below the window. Fell, apparently, but whether she threw herself out or someone pushed her, nobody knows. Restless spirit, though. There have been sightings ever since."

Sam listened, a sense of terrible foreboding settling inside him, giving him a sick, cold feeling as if he'd taken down a whole mouthful of ice cream in one big swallow.

"When . . . when there's a sighting," he asked, "what do people usually see?"

"Well, usually she's standing by the window, with her arms raised, like so."

"Come on, Dad!" Sam grabbed his father's arm, pulling him toward the museum's glass doors.

"What's the rush?" His father looked down at him, thoroughly puzzled.

"I'll explain in the car. We have to go!"

He knew where she was. He'd seen her come to the window. He'd been watching for most of the afternoon, hidden in the trees, waiting for them all to go. Different thoughts turned and twisted in his head, braiding themselves together until he knew what he would do. He couldn't let it go. Rejecting him like that. It was too humiliating. He'd show her. And her father. A tradesman's son. She thought he wasn't good enough. Well, he'd teach her. A thin smile curled. But he'd have his satisfaction first . . .

Tom didn't even question how he knew the staircase was there. He just did, that was all. He found the little door to the servants' passage at the base of the tower and crept up the winding stairway, feeling his way to the room where she'd be waiting, his shuffling feet scraping on the gritty stone.

Kate rocked back on her heels, surveying the words that she had just revealed.

NOW

A WARNING

GO

What could that mean? The words were at odds with the previous messages, perhaps signifying a new twist in the tale. Speculating about the possible story behind the phenomenon took some of the strangeness from it, made it seem less sinister. She stared at the wall, so completely absorbed in her thoughts that she heard nothing. His soft-soled footfalls were almost silent. Then there was a creaking sound from the corner, a tearing crack as wood broke through paper and he was there.

She leaped up, whirling around, the trowel in her hand clattering to the floor.

"How did you get there?!"

"There's more than one way up here." Tom grinned, shutting the secret door behind him. "I've been watching. Waiting for the others to go. For your dad and the brat to disappear. For a chance to be alone with you." He came across the room toward her, his tone changing to harshness. "I reckon we've got some unfinished business."

Kate moved away from him, backing toward the window. There was nowhere else to go.

"Careful." Tom gave a frown of feigned concern. "The frames are rotten, and so is the stone around them." He laughed. "That was my job for today."

Kate put her hand out, gripping the sill. It crumbled under her fingers like sand.

"This room's got a history. The whole house does. Didn't anyone tell you? S'pose not, or your dad never would have bought it."

He was close now, nearly upon her. She tried to make a break across the room.

"Don't even think about it." He grabbed her by the shoulder and pushed her back. "A young girl died. Here. In this room. It's a tragic story. Listen to me!" The thoughts were coming thick and fast, in no particular order. "She had a lover. They used to meet down in the summerhouse. One night she told him it was all over; she couldn't see him ever again. He followed her back here, not prepared to believe it. She wouldn't tell him why, but he guessed it. He knew her father was behind it, saying he wasn't good enough. He begged her, he pleaded, but she came across all haughty. Said she didn't love him, never had. He was a . . . a dalliance. A dalliance, merely. Hardhearted little bitch she turned out to be. Needed a lesson, see? She never should have done it. Never should have rejected—" He broke off, a muscle jumping in his cheek. "There was a fight. I don't know. Then she fell—fell from the window." A slight shudder ran through him. He paused to collect himself. "It doesn't have to be like that, does it? Not with you and me."

"I—I don't know . . ."

Kate shrank away from him. He was really scaring her. All that must have happened a long time ago, but he was talking as though he were there. She was right up against the window now. She felt the whole frame shifting in its mountings, bulging out, the rotting frame ready to crack.

"Yes, you do. You want me as much as I want you."

He was really close now. She could feel his breath hot on her, see his face sweating above her. She remembered how it had been in the car the night before, how hard it had been to resist him. He was so much stronger. His arms were reaching for her. She knew she wouldn't be able to fight him off a second time.

"Come on, Katie." His voice was muffled. "You know you want to."

He hadn't seen the chisel hidden behind her back. The blade was thin, the wedge-shaped tip razor sharp.

Then there was noise, her name being called. Light feet running, followed by a heavier, adult tread.

"Sam! Wait!" Her father's voice was shouting. "Leave it to me." He was right outside now. The door was opening. "Kate? Katie?"

Mark Banks found his daughter sitting under the window, the chisel still clutched in her hand. Tom Mayer's body lay stretched out beside her. Curls and shreds of wallpaper lay drifted about them, rustling like leaves on the bloodstained floor.

ENDINGS

Garth Nix

I have two swords. One is named Sorrow, and the other Joy. These are not their real names. I do not think there is anyone alive who knows even the letters that are etched into the blue-black blades.

I know, but then I am not alive. Yet not dead. Something in between, hovering in the twilight, betwixt wakefulness and sleep, caught on the boundary, pinned to the board, unable to go back, unable to go forward.

I do rest, but it is not sleep, and I do not dream. I simply remember, the memories tumbling over one another, mixing and joining and mingling till I do not know when or where or how or why, and by nightfall it is unbearable and I rise from my troubled bed to howl at the moon or pace the corridors.

Or sit beneath the swords in the old cane chair, waiting for the chance of a visitor, the chance of change, the chance . . .

I have two daughters. One is named Sorrow, and the other Joy.

These are not their real names. I do not think even they remember what they were called in the far-distant days of their youth. Neither they nor I can recall their mother's name, though sometimes in my daytime reveries I catch a glimpse of her face, the feel of her skin, the taste of her mouth, the swish of a sleeve as she leaves the room and my memory.

They are hungrier than I, my daughters, and still have the thirst for blood.

This story has two endings. One is named Sorrow, and the other Joy.

This is the first ending:

A great hero comes to my house without caution, as the sun falls. He is in the prime of life, tall and strong and arrogant. He meets my daughters in the garden, where they stand in the shade of the great oak. Two steps away lies the last sunlight, and he is clever enough to make use of that, and strong. There is pretended amour on both sides, and fangs strike true. Yet the hero is swifter with his silvered knife, and the sun is too close.

Silver poisons and fire burns, and that is the finish of Sorrow and the end of Joy.

Weakened, the hero staggers on, intent on finishing the epic that will be written about him. He finds me in the cane chair, and above me Sorrow and Joy.

I give him the choice and tell him the names.

He chooses Sorrow, not realizing that this is what he chooses for himself, and the blades are aptly named.

I do not feel sorrow for him, or for my daughters, but only for myself.

I do drink his blood. It has been a long time . . . and he was a hero.

This is the second ending:

A young man not yet old enough to be a hero, great or small, comes to my garden with the dawn. He watches me through the window, and though I delay, at last I must shuffle out of the cane chair, toward my bed.

There are bones at my feet, and a skull, the flesh long gone. I do not know whose bones they are. There are many skulls and bones about this house.

The boy enters through the window, borne on a shaft of sunlight. I pause in the shadowed doorway to watch as he examines the swords. His lips move, puzzling out what is written there, or so I must suppose. Perhaps no alphabet or language is ever really lost, as long as some of it survives.

He will get no help from that ancient script, from that ancient life.

I call out the names I have given the swords, but he does not answer.

I do not see which weapon he chooses. Already memories rush at me, push at me, buffet and surround me. I do not know what has happened or will happen or might happen.

I am in my bed. The youth stands over me, the point of a sword pricking at my chest.

It is Joy, and I think chosen through wisdom, not by luck. Who would have thought it of a boy not yet old enough to shave?

The steel is cold. Final. Yet only dust bubbles from the wound.

Then comes the second blow, to the dry bones of the neck.

I have been waiting a long time for this ending.

Waiting for someone to choose for me.

To give me Joy, instead of Sorrow.

※

ABOUT THE AUTHORS

JOAN AIKEN was born in Sussex to American poet Conrad Aiken and Canadian Jessie McDonald Aiken, and died on January 4, 2004, at the age of seventy-nine, having written more than one hundred books for young readers and adults. Perhaps her best-known books for children are the Wolves Chronicles, which began with the classic *The Wolves of Willoughby Chase*, for which she won the Lewis Carroll Award. Her novels are internationally acclaimed, and among other honors, she was a recipient of the Edgar Allan Poe Award in the United States and the *Guardian* Award in England.

Of her short story "Lungewater," Joan Aiken said, "I wrote this story about four years ago after reading an article in a countryside magazine about a famous fishing river in a county next to the one where I live in England. The river narrows into dramatic rapids at one point and runs between two cliffs. The gap is rather too wide to jump except for Olympic-standard athletes. But every now and then some intrepid local lad attempts it, sometimes with disastrous results. I have not seen this place myself, as it is in a private estate, but I was fascinated by the description and felt that, if not haunted already (as it probably is), it deserves to have a ghost story written about it. So I wrote one."

M. T. ANDERSON has published three novels for teens, most recently *Feed*—a National Book Award Finalist, a *Boston Globe–Horn Book* Honor Award winner, and winner of the *Los Angeles Times* Book Award. The plot of "Watch and Wake" is an ancient one, taken from the Roman author Apuleius's mystical book *The Golden Donkey*, written around A.D. 150. "It's your basic boy-meets-witch, 'Who's got your nose?' story," says Anderson. He set the modern retelling in the same world as his first novel, *Thirsty*, "a world where Americana has become occult, and the suburbs are full of rituals." He currently lives in Boston and teaches writing at Vermont College.

NEIL GAIMAN is the author of nonfiction, radio plays, comics, and screenplays in addition to his highly acclaimed fiction. His books include *American Gods, Neverwhere, Coraline, The Wolves in the Walls,* and many classic graphic novels, among them twelve volumes of *The Sandman.* He has won three Bram Stoker Awards, one World Fantasy Award, a Nebula, two Hugos, three Locus Awards, and sundry others. "They look nice on the windowsills," he says, "next to the things I get from the Disturbing Bunny of the Month Club." Neil Gaiman was born in England and would "like to die in England," although he has lived in the United States for more than a decade now, most recently "in a gloomy Victorian house with a tower."

Of "Forbidden Brides of the Faceless Slaves in the Nameless House of the Night of Dread Desire," he says, "I wrote my first draft of this story a very long time ago and made the mistake of showing it to someone who didn't get it and didn't like it and told me so. I listened to people more back then, and I put it away, ashamed. So the story waited in the darkness for a long time for me to pull it out, and read it, and smile, and do the second draft it had been waiting for. I love the true gothics and the faux gothics, and any book with a lady in a nightdress holding a candelabra and running away from an old dark house on the cover. This story's really a sort of love letter to them, and to the imagination."

CAITLÍN R. KIERNAN is the author of four novels, including the award-winning *Silk* and *Threshold*, and her short fiction has been collected in three volumes: *Tales of Pain and Wonder*; *From Weird and Distant Shores*; and *To Charles Fort, With Love*. Starling Jane, the central character of "The Dead and the Moonstruck," first

appears in Kiernan's most recent novel, *Low Red Moon*.
"In the novel, Jane's a teenager," says the author, "so
this was an opportunity for me to revisit her as a
child. And I wanted to do a coming-of-age, rites-of-
passage sort of story in a dark and alien culture."
Caitlín R. Kiernan lives in Atlanta.

GREGORY MAGUIRE is the author of more than a
dozen novels for young readers, including the popular Hamlet Chronicles. He has also written four novels for adults, the most recent being *Mirror Mirror*. His
novel *Wicked*, about the Wicked Witch of the West
from *The Wizard of Oz*, is the basis of the Broadway
musical of the same name. In the early 1990s Maguire
visited the castle of Vlad Dracul in Romania—and
refers briefly to that visit in his adult novel *Lost*—but
he was bitten by nothing more than an urge to tell a
faintly creepier story than he'd attempted previously.
"The Prank" is one such effort. Gregory Maguire lives
in Massachusetts.

GARTH NIX is the award-winning author of several
books for young readers, including *Sabriel*, an ALA
Notable Book, a New York Public Library Book for the
Teen Age, and the 1995 winner of Australia's Aurealis
Award for Best Fantasy Novel and Best Young Adult

Novel; *Lirael*, an ALA Best Book for Young Adults; *Shade's Children*, an ALA Best Book for Young Adults; the *New York Times* and *Publishers Weekly* bestseller *Abhorsen*; and the Seventh Tower series.

Of "Endings," he says, "I found it while I was walking one evening in the cemetery on the hill above my office. A woman in white fled beyond the gravestones, pursued by laughing shadows. Near my feet, a skeletal hand held a scroll. I took the scroll as the bones crumbled to dust, and fled myself, back to the harsh white light of the suburban streets." Garth Nix lives in Sydney.

CELIA REES has written many books for teens, including the acclaimed *Witch Child* and *Sorceress*. *Witch Child* was an ALA Best Book for Young Adults, a Book Sense 76 Top Ten Pick, a New York Public Library Book for the Teen Age, a Borders Original Voices nominee, an IRA Young Adults' Choice, and was shortlisted for the *Guardian* Children's Book Award. *Sorceress* was a Book Sense 76 Selection and was shortlisted for the Whitbread Children's Book Award.

Of "Writing on the Wall," the author says, "I love real ghost stories, about actual places and things that people believe really happened. If I'm writing this kind of fiction, that is where I go for inspiration. Certain places, certain houses, have gained a reputation for supernatural events. Happenings that had to be guarded against in all sorts of ways: by carving hex signs, concealing witch bottles, or even cats, building them into the fabric of the dwelling. 'Writing on the Wall' is about such a house." Celia Rees lives in Warwickshire.

JANNI LEE SIMNER lives in the hot, bright, and not-at-all-gothic Arizona desert. Her short stories have appeared in more than two dozen anthologies and magazines, including *Bruce Coville's Book of Nightmares, Ghosts and Golems, Not of Woman Born,* and *Half Human.* She's also author of a forthcoming middle-grade mystery. "When I started writing 'Stone Tower,'" she says, "I had no more idea than Tara how she'd come to be imprisoned; I had to write the story to find out. That sense of the threatening unknown is, I think, at the heart of many gothic tales."

VIVIAN VANDE VELDE is the author of more than twenty books, mostly science fiction and fantasy for middle-grade readers and teens—including *Heir Apparent,* winner of the Anne Spencer Lindbergh Prize in Children's Literature; *Never Trust a Dead Man,* winner of the 2000 Young Adult Edgar Award; *Alison, Who Went Away; Witch's Wishes;* and *Ghost of a Hanged Man.* Of

"Morgan Roehmar's Boys," she says, "Halloween is a time of disguises, of people or things pretending to be something they're not. So there, on someone's porch, is a bundle of stuffed clothes, a dummy, propped up to look like a spooky old woman; and there, hanging from that porch rafter, is another dummy that looks like a corpse. Or at least you assume they're just dummies . . ." Vivian Vande Velde lives in Rochester, New York.

BARRY YOURGRAU's adult books include *Wearing Dad's Head*. He starred in *The Sadness of Sex*, a movie adaptation of his stories, and has performed on MTV and NPR. His debut for young readers is the middle-grade fantasy *My Curious Uncle Dudley*. Barry's "Crumpot" saga here teases a Walter Mitty theme (a poor sap who's heroic in his fantasies) with some wicked vampirish jolts. "I like the funny side of fright," says Barry. "Since I'm myself scared of the dark, of big lonely houses, of horror movies, I must salute my protagonist, poor Walter. He's braver than I am." Barry Yourgrau trembles in New York.